Also by Corey Ann Haydu
Rules for Stealing Stars
The Someday Suitcase

EVENTOWN

Corey Ann Haydu

KATHERINE TEGEN BOOKS
An Imprint of HarperCollins Publishers

Katherine Tegen Books is an imprint of HarperCollins Publishers.

Library of Congress Cataloging-in-Publication Data

Names: Haydu, Corey Ann, author.
Title: Eventown / Corey Ann Haydu.
Description: First edition. | New York, NY : Katherine Tegen Books, an imprint of
    HarperCollinsPublishers, [2019] | Summary: To Elodee, eleven, things seem a little
    too perfect in Eventown when she moves there with her parents and identical twin,
    Naomi, especially since forgetting the past is so highly valued.
Identifiers: LCCN 2018013964 | ISBN 9780062689801 (hardback)
Subjects: | CYAC: Memory—Fiction. | Conformity—Fiction. | City and town
    life—Fiction. | Sisters—Fiction. | Twins—Fiction. | Family life—Fiction. | Moving,
    Household—Fiction.
Classification: LCC PZ7.H31389 Eve 2019 | DDC [Fic]—dc23 LC record available at
    https://lccn.loc.gov/2018013964

Typography by Aurora Parlagreco
18 19 20 21 22 CG/LSCH 10 9 8 7 6 5 4 3 2 1
❖
First Edition

To my editor, Alex,
who helps my sparks turn into stories.
And so, so much more.

1

Fresh Start

Jenny Horowitz likes horses and the color pink and asking lots of questions about things I don't want to talk about. Today she's got one of her favorite horse T-shirts on, a pink one, and she's asking me about The Move, even though every time she mentions it I turn to Naomi and ask a question about multiplying fractions, which we're learning about in math class. Jenny, Bess, and Flora should all know that if I'm talking about multiplying fractions, I must *really* not want to talk about The Move.

Of the two of us, Naomi is the harder twin to read. I love talking, but she's quiet all the time—when she's happy or sad or scared or anything else. I can see the little differences.

When she's happy she blushes, and when she's sad she stares out windows, and when she's scared she leans in close to me, like I might protect her.

And I would. I would try to protect Naomi from just about anything.

I'm just not so sure who's going to protect *me* when we're in our new town.

"Do you think the other kids will like you?" Jenny asks. "Are the kids different there? Mom says everything's different there."

"What's one-fifth times two-fifths?" I ask my identical twin sister. Naomi shrugs even though I'd bet anything she knows the answer. She looks up at the ceiling and crosses her arms. She is angry, but no one else can tell.

When I'm angry, everyone knows it.

And I'm starting to get angry right now.

Naomi sees it and gives me a look that reminds me to act normal. Naomi and I have found that if you act normal when you're out in public, you can save all your sad and sorry and worried feelings for home.

At home, when it's just us, we do a lot of being sad and sorry and worried.

But at school Naomi is That Amazing Gymnast and I am The Girl Who Makes Weird Cookies and we are both in The Group of Girls Who Most People Pretty Much Like.

Lately, though, I've been having a harder time pretending to be The Girl Who Most People Pretty Much Like (Even Though She's a Little Loud and a Little Weird Sometimes). I know I'm supposed to be Elodee from Before and Naomi is supposed to be Naomi from Before, because otherwise we have to be something much, much worse.

Still, it's hard to be from Before when you are in Now. I am not doing the best job at it. Last week, I yelled at Jon in the middle of English class. I used a bad word. One of the only words Dad says we can't use. I said it right in front of the teacher.

I got in trouble of course, but Jon did, too, because everyone heard what he said to me. It was something very, very mean.

It made Naomi sad. Things that make me angry often make Naomi sad, and that's the part of being twins no one really understands. Especially me.

"Why are you moving in March?" Jenny asks. "Shouldn't you wait until the summer and move then?"

"What about dividing fractions?" I ask Naomi. "Is that even harder than multiplying?"

Naomi nods. "Dividing is really hard," she says. She looks out a window and I know the sentence has made her sad. I wish she could get angry with me instead.

"Have you even seen your new house? Have your *parents*

even seen it? Don't you have to see a house before you move into it?" Jenny is relentless. She's speaking so loudly that other people are turning and looking at us, and no amount of shushing from Bess or nudging from Flora seems to be stopping her.

"Fractions are weird. I like regular full numbers better," I say.

"Me too," Naomi says. I'm running out of things to say about multiplying fractions, and I'm hot under my arms and all over my chest.

Flora and Bess are exchanging glances that they think I don't notice, but I do. I notice the way they roll their eyes at the weird things I do and the way they sometimes lean away from me like they don't want other, more popular girls, more normal girls, to know that we are friends.

What they don't know is that I don't care about any of that anymore.

What they don't know is that it's Jenny who is being awful by not stopping her question asking when I obviously don't want to answer. I am angry at all of them with their tiny, almost-invisible dismissals and the not-so-tiny ways they tell us that they want everything to go back to the way it was before, not because they want us to be less sad, but because they want their own lives to be easier.

Sometimes I'm so angry at my friends I wonder if I

even have room for other things like sadness and happiness anymore.

I wonder why Jenny can't see it, simmering under my skin. Pricking my eyes, making me sweat.

"I heard my mom talking to my dad, and she says it's really good you guys are leaving and you should have left right away because your family really needs a fresh start so that you can be okay again and leaving here is the best way for you to do that."

It happens so fast, I could almost pretend it didn't happen at all.

I shove Jenny Horowitz against the wall. My hands press hard into her shoulders, my elbows bend, and I let it all go—The Move, the last few months, Jenny's stupid horse shirt, the fact that Naomi's a gymnastics star and I can't do a cartwheel, Bess's birthday party last month where she invited Flora and Jenny to sleep over but didn't ask me and Naomi, the way my shoes pinch because I need a new pair and Mom keeps forgetting, Dad's bad moods, Jenny's incessant questions, the way people say the words *fresh start* and how it sounds more like a threat or a punishment than some great goal to work toward, Naomi's quietness getting even quieter, and everything else that's made the last few months feel like something I'm carrying around and not something I'm moving through.

5

With all that going into the push, it's a wonder Jenny doesn't fly right through the wall, into the janitor's closet on the other side.

Instead, her glasses—pink, of course—fall from her face, and her shoulders meet the wall with a thump, and the other kids around us gasp, their hands over their mouths and their eyes moon-wide, like cartoon characters instead of real people.

It takes about one second for Ms. Marley to rush to the scene, as if she knew something like this was going to happen.

I didn't know, though. I never seem to know what's coming.

It didn't feel good, shoving Jenny. It didn't feel good calling Jon the bad word, either. It felt inevitable, though.

Sometimes I think feelings are bigger than people. More powerful. They make people do things that can't be undone. I used to think feelings were part of a person, but lately I've been thinking they are separate beings, that they come like aliens and invade people's bodies and cause destruction.

Naomi didn't agree or disagree when I told her my theory. But I heard her sniffling in the top bunk later that night, and I thought, *Yep, there's an alien, taking over Naomi's body for the night. What a jerk.*

After shoving Jenny, I sit in the principal's office and

make fists with my hands and keep all my muscles very, very tense. Sometimes I hang my head and take deep breaths, but I don't cry and I don't yell and I definitely don't shove anyone else.

The principal doesn't get mad at me. She doesn't punish me since it's my last day of school anyway.

I have always liked the principal. She wears dresses with cat patterns and bird patterns and giraffe patterns, and she makes goofy jokes that kids make fun of but I sort of like. She has never treated me any differently than she did last year.

"Some days are harder than other days," she says with a sigh, like she knows the same things I know, like she's shoved someone, too, like she's sat in a little room like this one and gotten a headache from the effort of trying to be okay. "Isn't that right, Miss Lively?"

I don't say anything. I don't make any noise at all. But I nod at the way a principal in a dress covered in elephants can say something so simple and so true.

2

The Only Pretty Thing in Jupiter

The next morning, our last full day in Juniper, I help Dad in the yard with the rosebush.

The rosebush is the prettiest thing in all of Juniper. It might be one of the only truly pretty things here, in fact. Bess thinks the glass elevator at the mall is pretty and Flora thinks the skyscrapers we can see from the highway are pretty and Jenny thinks the big white houses in the center of town are pretty, but I'm not so sure about any of that.

"Are there roses where we're going?" I ask Dad while he grunts and digs and gently touches the reddest petals.

"You remember," he says. "There are roses everywhere in Eventown. You said it was prettier than Juniper could ever be. You're the one who said you wanted to live there."

I do remember. I remember everything, because when something happens I turn it over and over and over in my head a thousand times until I am sure I understand it. And sometimes I make a cake or a cookie or even a pot roast based on the thing that happened. When Mom got her new job offer with Eventown tourism, I made a celebration vanilla cake with confetti sprinkles on top but a confused strawberry-raspberry-peanut-butter center. When I called Jon the bad word, I made apology cookies with bitter coffee bits inside. When Bess "forgot" to invite us to sleep over after her party, I made spicy, angry pasta with lots of chili pepper and even a dash of Tabasco in the sauce and jalapeño bread instead of garlic bread. For dessert I made the sweetest chocolate pudding with the fluffiest marshmallow whipped cream because Dad said even the angriest days can have sweet moments.

"If there are so many rosebushes there, why do we have to bring this one with us?" I ask. I love this rosebush, but I also feel a little sad about taking away the only pretty thing in Juniper. Once this rosebush is gone, the prettiest thing in Juniper will probably be the pond over by Flora's house, but it's an ugly brown color and slimy when you stick your feet in. I always look for goldfish in there—a flash of orange would make the pond so much nicer. But there are only ever tadpoles.

"It's the family rosebush," Dad says. "We can't leave

without it." He's sweating onto the handle of his shovel, onto the ground, onto his shoes. From inside, Mom and Naomi watch, Mom shaking her head and Naomi with the look on her face that she's had for weeks—like she's thinking too hard but no thoughts are coming.

I have my own shovel and a pair of gloves Dad gave me for Christmas. I don't love gardening and dirt the way he does, but I like the smell of flowers and grass and the way Dad's face relaxes when he's out here, his worried eyes un-worrying themselves, his fists turning back into regular hands.

Plus, I have to be extra-helpful after the Jenny Incident. When Mom and Dad got off the phone with the principal, they didn't punish me or yell at me or even talk to me about what had happened. Mom sighed and handed me a cardboard box and told me to start packing up the kitchen. Dad said he'd need help in the garden. I, of course, didn't argue with either of them.

Still, it's strange to do something so big and not get in any trouble for it. Lately everything Naomi and I do is okay. Even when what we do really, really isn't okay. Parents and teachers and all the adults in Juniper seem nervous around us. Like it would be dangerous to get too mad at us.

Even Mom and Dad don't have much to say to us anymore. It feels like there's a list of things we aren't supposed to talk about or even think about or feel, and I'm trying my hardest not to talk or think about any of them. Not even with Naomi. Not even with myself.

But it's not easy.

It's uncomfortable, like the whole world tilted just the tiniest bit to the right and gravity and all the other laws of the universe aren't working quite right anymore.

The world did tilt, I guess.

We almost fell off the edge, I think.

I shiver, not wanting to think about tilting worlds or the principal's sad-pitying-nervous face.

I gesture at Naomi to come outside, waving my hands. Naomi sticks her tongue out at me. I stick my tongue out at her. She gets a look on her face that's filled with mischief, and before the look fades, she disappears below the window frame. A moment later, her feet are in the window, dancing and wiggling in the air.

It makes me laugh.

In the midst of everything, Naomi can still make me laugh. She turns herself back around, and when her face is back in sight, it's red and beaming.

"Your turn," she mouths. This is the Naomi no one else really sees. She doesn't like other people seeing that she's goofy and silly and funny. She keeps it all locked up, and I'm the person who gets to see it.

Still, I wish I had someone to be silly with out in the world.

I put my hands on the ground and fling my feet in the air. They fling themselves right back down. It hurts and I'm muddy and grass stained, but Naomi's laughing and I'm laughing and it's a joke that no one else thinks is funny but us.

Which makes it the best kind of joke there is.

Every once in a while, Naomi and I make each other laugh, and it almost feels like everything might be okay again someday.

Maybe in Eventown, it will be.

I start to shovel alongside Dad. He grunts every time his shovel hits the earth. At one point he takes off his glove and gets stuck by a thorn. He leaps away from the pain and laughs at himself. He's always saying, *Elodee, roses are fickle. They require care and seriousness. Their thorns can hurt you. Their petals can wilt. But if you do everything right, they're beautiful.*

It sounds like a lot of pressure to me, which is partly why I don't love gardening so much. It's too precarious—that's a word we learned a few weeks ago. It means things might fall apart at any second, if you're not careful. Sometimes, things are precarious and you don't even know it.

I didn't know the word *precarious* earlier this year, but I wish I had. It would have explained a lot.

With gardening, no matter how hard you try, you might do something the tiniest bit wrong and ruin everything. Dad tried to teach Naomi and me to be gardeners, but we weren't very good. We planted wallflowers once, and watered them all the time, but wallflowers hate lots of water. We tried ferns next, and spritzed them every few days with Dad's little spray bottle, but the ferns dried up, begging for more. I wanted to keep trying more plants, but it made Naomi too sad, to mess up like that.

Naomi's always afraid of messing up.

I'm not like that at all. I mess up a lot. In the kitchen, messing up's okay. Things aren't so precarious. I can add peppers when it says to add tomatoes or cilantro when it calls for basil. Mostly, I don't even use recipes, I just play with what's on the Elodee shelf in the kitchen and hope it turns into something delicious.

Last week, we had a bunch of potatoes and avocados and eggs. I made a delicious scramble for everyone for breakfast and found chives and garlic to put on top. It seemed almost too simple, so I took a look at the Elodee shelf to see if I'd collected anything that might fit in.

"It's good as it is," Naomi said, annoyed that she had to wait to eat her breakfast.

"It's boring," I said. "I know I can make it better." I found cumin and jalapeños and a fancy blood orange olive oil on

13

the Elodee shelf, and I made a sort of salsa for the eggs.

Naomi wouldn't even try it.

Mom nibbled.

But Dad and I knew it made the meal something better than breakfast. It made breakfast an adventure.

I wish I felt as sure about the adventure we have coming up now as I did about the crazy salsa.

"Is there a mall in Eventown?" I ask. "Is there an Olive Garden and a McDonald's and a train station that the big kids hang out at?"

Dad doesn't answer. He just sighs. He sighs at everything lately. Overcooked eggs and coffee that's a little too hot and the weather, even if it's seventy and sunny. He sighs at Mom's efforts to have fun—movie night, pizza night, pottery night, yoga night.

The rosebush and Eventown are the only things Dad seems happy about. Not happy like the old days, but his new happy. Old happy had goofy made-up songs and air-guitar and a silly smile with his tongue inching out. New happy really only means Dad isn't grumpy. New happy is quiet and closed mouth almost-smiles and a different sigh—a relieved one instead of a tired one.

"Help me with this side, Elodee," Dad says. "But be gentle. The root's the most important part."

I nod and go to Dad's side, but I'm uneasy about unearthing the beautiful plant.

Dad prepares a transfer bed for the bush, a place where the plant will go as it travels from the place we've always lived to the new place, where we've only ever visited once before.

When Dad needs a break, I take one, too, and finally Naomi joins me outside.

"Are you all packed?" Naomi asks, sounding like Mom.

"Yeah. It's weird not having anything in the dresser anymore."

"I don't know what to bring. Do you think they dress the same in Eventown? Do you remember?"

"I think so?" We stayed in Eventown for a weekend two years ago, the whole family, and it was the best weekend of my life. And everyone else's. There's an amazing ice cream shop in the center of town, with new flavors every day. There are rosebushes everywhere, and hills on all sides, perfect for hikes that lead to waterfalls or fields for picnicking or gardens of more roses in even more colors. Here in Juniper, I don't like hiking at all. My shoulders get cold while my feet get hot. Bugs bite my thighs and dirt gets in my eyes and the end of the hike only ever leads us back to the beginning.

In Eventown, I loved hiking. It was somehow always the perfect temperature, and the view at the end was always worth it.

"Pack stuff for hiking," I tell Naomi. "Do you remember yelling all our secrets at the top of that one hill? We have

15

to do that again." It was one of the best days in Eventown. The air felt so good and the top of the hill felt so far away from everything that we screamed out secrets at the tops of our lungs. Then a family of hikers came up right behind us and we all giggled, knowing that they'd heard about who Naomi had a crush on and what I really thought of our music teacher and a bunch of other secrets that no one was supposed to actually hear.

Naomi was so embarrassed she threw the picnic blanket over her head, but I didn't mind one bit. I had learned by then that it wasn't so bad when people thought you were strange.

"Being weird is the same as being brave," I'd been told. It felt especially true that day, so I told Naomi. She didn't really agree. She still doesn't. So I try to be brave and weird enough for both of us.

It's not as fun as being brave and weird with someone else.

"I don't have hiking stuff," Naomi says. "I don't want to go." I guess she's not remembering the same things I am. We have the same almost-red-but-really-actually-brown hair and pale freckly skin, the same extra-brown eyes and sharp elbows and crooked front teeth, but sometimes we forget to be the same in all the most important ways.

"Maybe it will be fun," I say. "Maybe Mom and Dad

will like it. Remember when we visited, how they danced at dinner, how they let us stay up late to play board games, how no one got burned at the beach?"

"I remember," Naomi says.

"Remember how when we visited you finally perfected a back handspring and I made a cake that didn't fall and everything smelled like roses?"

Naomi nods. I'm not sure about the move either, but Mom and Dad want us to be positive about it, and I want Mom and Dad to be happy, so I work on my smile and a chipper voice and hope Naomi comes around too. I focus on all those happy Eventown memories and hope that maybe, *maybe*, living there will be as good as visiting was.

"What are you going to miss most?" I ask. I'm thinking maybe if I know what it is, I can make sure we have it in Eventown. Saturdays at the mall, the same strip of duct tape across our bedroom for her to practice her beam routine on; I'll even let her keep the top bunk and I'll stay on the bottom one.

Naomi starts to cry, and I know what that means. I scoot closer to her and it feels like I could cry, too, but I work hard not to. Naomi and I promised that we'd be sad one at a time, so that there's never too much sadness in one place. I make all the room in the world for Naomi's tears now. I don't even let myself sniffle from all the things I might miss too.

Naomi walks over to the rosebush. She peers into the hole we've dug.

"Careful!" I say. Naomi's clumsy everywhere except the gym, and I'm terrified of her hurting Dad's plant. I get the feeling that if something happened to the rosebush, Dad might not even be able to muster New Happy for a long, long time.

"I'm careful."

"The roots are the most important part," I say in my teacher voice. I am six minutes older than Naomi, and that means sometimes I get to boss her around. This time, though, Naomi doesn't even roll her eyes. She sits on the ground, staring at the plant, half in the ground, half out. It's getting overcast and it might rain, which will make getting the rosebush out even harder, but I know Dad will find a way. Naomi looks this way and that, trying to see all angles of the plant—the flowers, the roots, the thorns, the exact angle it's set in the ground.

"If roots are so important," Naomi says at last, "why are we moving ours around?"

3

Moving Day

Mom and Dad are packing up every room in the house but one, the green stripy one at the end of the hall.

I don't notice the one not-packed room until Sunday morning, when we're almost ready to go.

"We don't need to bring any of that with us," Mom says, and I guess that's the end of the discussion because no one argues with her about it. We close the door.

The house is dusty once we move things around, and Naomi can't stop sneezing. I'm trying to sweep the living room floor, but her sneezes keep startling me into dropping my broom. Naomi's sneezes are high pitched and impossible to ignore. Some days it's funny, but today, Moving Day, I can't stand it.

"Why aren't we bringing the TV?" Naomi asks, before another enormous sneeze zooms out of her.

"Stop with all the sneezing!" I say.

"I can't!"

"Yes, you can! Hold it in!"

"You're not supposed to hold in sneezes. It's dangerous."

"That's a myth."

"Achoo!"

"Oh my GOD."

"Shut up, Elodee. People sneeze."

"You shut up!"

"GIRLS." Dad's the one to finally interrupt us, not Mom, who is checking things off on an enormous pad of yellow legal paper. She has her fancy purple pen and her reading glasses perched on her nose and a very serious look on her face. She counts things out on her fingers and scans the room over and over.

"Sorry," Naomi and I mumble together. She's my best friend in the world, but we fight at least once a day. Sometimes it's about little stuff like sneezes or snores or the last cookie in the jar, and sometimes it's about bigger things, like who is closer friends with Bess Patrickson or who Mom and Dad are easier on.

"We don't need to bring the TV," Mom says, finally answering Naomi's question.

"We don't? There's one there?" I say.

"Nope." Mom smiles. I haven't seen Mom's smile much lately, so I want to grab it from her face and put it in my pocket, for safekeeping.

"I don't get it," Naomi says.

Dad gives Mom a Look, one that says she should stop talking or change the subject or offer us sundaes as distraction, but Mom doesn't notice the Look.

"No one watches TV in Eventown. Don't you girls remember that?"

Naomi and I wait for Mom to laugh or Dad to roll his eyes. They don't. Dad looks at his hands and Mom smiles like no TV is the normalest thing in the world.

I hadn't remembered that we didn't watch TV in Eventown, but I guess we didn't. I know that Naomi and I read a bunch of books we'd brought from home—a whole series about a girl pirate and another one about firefighting cats. We loved them both. Maybe Mom's right. I don't recall a movie night while we were there or hours of cartoons or even Mom and Dad watching the news and telling us to play outside.

I wonder if there's a movie theater in Eventown. The one in Juniper has sticky leather seats and smells like day-old popcorn and only ever plays movies with lots of cars and shooting and earthquakes and cartoon princesses. I won't miss any of that, but once a year, on Christmas Eve, Mom and Dad take us to a midnight movie and we eat gingerbread in the back row and talk loud about nothing because no one else is sharing the theater with us.

I guess I'd miss that one night a year. But you don't stay in a town with a depressing movie theater just for that one night a year.

I open my mouth to ask about Christmas Eve and Eventown movie theaters, but Naomi's still stuck on the television.

"No TV ever?" Naomi's voice is small and wavering, but Mom doesn't notice.

"Not ever!" Mom says.

"What about internet?" Naomi says.

"None of that either!" Mom says. "Just a computer in the library for research and emergencies!"

It's a lot to take in.

"It'll be okay, girls," Dad says. That's what he says all the time now, about things that are most definitely not okay. Dad seems to think that if he says things will be okay, we'll suddenly feel better. We try to make that be true, but it really, really isn't.

I haven't thought to look around to see what else we aren't bringing, but I do it now with Naomi, running from room to room to see what's left behind. Mom's not bringing her old-timey record player or all the records she's collected over the years, making us stop at yard sales in the middle of nowhere to check out what they're selling for a dollar a record. She's leaving behind shelves of books and a bunch of framed photographs of the family and a big quilt that Aunt March made us when we were babies. She's leaving behind all of our winter coats and hats and scarves, our silver sled, and a painting of the sun that has been in our living room forever.

"Why aren't we bringing all our stuff?" I ask when we're back in the living room with the piles of boxes and sheepish Dad and cheerful Mom.

"Oh, Bess's mom is going to run a nice yard sale to get rid of some of it, and the new people who bought the house want to keep a lot of our other stuff. We don't need to drag it along. The house in Eventown is all furnished and ready for us!"

"I don't want to go," Naomi whisper-whines.

I yell for the both of us. "We're not going! We're not leaving our home!"

"We're starting over," Mom says. She won't be shaken up. She's refusing. "It's for the best."

"There will still be gymnastics for you, Naomi, and a beautiful kitchen for you, Elodee, and lots of gardening for me," Dad says.

"What's Mom bringing for her?" I ask. I noticed her

computer has been left behind, the book she was working on presumably abandoned too.

"Eventown is for me," Mom says. "I won't need anything else."

4

My Favorite Naomi

Bess Patrickson lives a few houses away from us, and she comes by to say goodbye, along with Flora Alvarez and a pouty, nervous Jenny Horowitz. They must have all slept over at Bess's house last night. They have that sleepover look—nails painted the same color and sleepy eyes and a thousand new inside jokes trembling between them.

They stand in a line and offer us one hug each and a card with all their signatures on it. Jenny drew hers with a heart. Flora wrote hers bigger than the rest, as if we might otherwise miss it. And Bess wrote us both a little note about how much she'll miss us. The five of us stand in the driveway and talk about things that won't matter the instant we leave town. The math test last week. Jenny's cute shoes. What we had for dinner the night before. It's almost like we're already gone, living different lives before our car even pulls away.

It begins to drizzle. The only person with an umbrella is Bess, so we all huddle under it.

Except Naomi. It drives Mom crazy, but Naomi *likes* standing in the rain. She'll come in from a rainy day soaking wet, her clothes ruined, her hair messy and dripping, her mouth in a breakfast-for-dinner smile.

"Get under here," Jenny orders, but Naomi's not having it.

"And miss all this?" she says, spreading her arms wide and letting the drizzle become a downpour right on top of her head. It's the only thing Naomi does that no one else does, a part of her that is weird and magical. Mostly Naomi wants to do what everyone else does. She likes fitting in.

I guess it takes loving the rain so, so much to make her stop caring what everyone else thinks. Naomi in the rain, not caring about what other people think is my favorite Naomi, so I wish for rain a lot, especially lately.

"Weirdo," Jenny says with an eye roll. She has called me that same word a lot of times before. Sometimes I think that if I didn't have Naomi, none of them would be friends with me at all. They prefer the way Naomi wears her hair in a shiny ponytail and that she's quiet and polite with parents and teachers. They like that she laughs at their jokes and wears normal, boring outfits and buys the same brand of raspberry soap and jeans and monogrammed backpack as everyone else.

Naomi is not the weirdo. She never has been. So it sounds especially sharp when Jenny calls her one. Naomi doesn't notice. She's smelling the rain. To me it smells like nothing, like air. But Naomi says it smells a little grassy and a little springy and a little like wonder. When I asked what kind of cake she wanted me to try to make for our twelfth birthday this spring, she said she'd like a rain-flavored one.

I haven't been able to figure that mystery out yet. Maybe in Eventown.

Under the umbrella, we do not talk about what happened yesterday at school. Still, Jenny won't meet my gaze. Her glasses seem intact, luckily, and I bet she's been counting down the seconds until we're all the way out of Juniper.

"Mom says Eventown is the perfect place for you to go," Flora says. "She read an article about it. Everyone who lives there loves it."

"My dad said that too," Bess says. "He said it's not the kind of place *we* would ever go because it's sort of a weird place? But he said you guys need a change."

Jenny looks at the ground and nods. Naomi crosses her arms over her chest and focuses on the rain hitting her skin.

27

I have never been so aware of adults talking about me and my family and our decisions. It freaks me out.

"Well, he's wrong," I snap. "Eventown's normal, and we don't need a change anyway."

"I'm trying to be nice," Bess says.

"We're all being nice," Jenny says. "We've all *been* nice." She gestures to their card, like it's something really special and impressive. It's not.

"We try so hard and you guys don't try at all," Flora says. I feel yesterday's anger bubbling again. It's clear from the way they're speaking that they've had a zillion conversations about Naomi and me and how not-fun and not-happy and not-the-same we've been these last few months. I scoot closer to Naomi. Away from the umbrella. I'd rather have her to hold on to. I need to be protected from our friends more than I need to be shielded from the rain.

The rain comes down harder, and I'm drenched in a moment, but it's worth it to be close to my twin.

"Sounds like you all will be just fine without us," I say, and Naomi nods.

"We came to say goodbye! We brought the card!" Bess says. "Even after everything that happened this week!"

"Probably because your parents told you to," Naomi says, and as soon as she says it I know it's true. A year ago, Bess would have been here because she wanted to be, because she

28

couldn't imagine life without us, because she needed to weep into our arms and wave as we pulled out of the driveway. A year ago, we'd have had plans to be pen pals, to visit over summer break, to call and text each other all the time.

Today, Bess, Jenny, and Flora exchange a look that confirms exactly what Naomi just said. Their parents made them come. As soon as they leave they'll probably walk to the mall and try on lip gloss at the makeup counter before eating pretzels by the fountain.

"You're not going to miss us," I say. All three girls look at each other and then at their feet, and I know it's true. They'll be relieved that they can stop worrying about us, stop checking in on us when their parents tell them to, stop trying to make us laugh when we don't feel like it.

"You guys have each other, at least," Bess says. "When I moved here I was all by myself." She shrugs, like that's the final word on our big move. The other girls nod, too, and squirm. They want to leave. They wish we were already gone.

"Sure," Naomi and I say in unison. It's a true and not-true statement. It's good, to have each other. But it doesn't mean we don't need anyone else.

I don't care much about the rain and I'm too loud for Naomi. Naomi doesn't like cooking or baking or even really eating my finished projects. She likes pizza and chicken parmesan and French fries and not much else. She wrinkles her nose at spices and new flavors and the way the kitchen smells after I've been messing around in it all day. She rolls her eyes when I sing in public or wear a tutu to school or ask too many questions when I meet strangers.

Naomi wants to be quiet when she's sad and I want to be loud, and we're not very good at cheering each other up. I didn't notice, before. But now that we're all we have, it's pretty obvious what we're missing.

"Cool. Well. Good luck!" Jenny says. It's funny, I would have said Bess was the leader of our group, but it looks like Jenny is now. Maybe I shoved her into a new position of power. She shakes her hair over her shoulders and applies a layer of scented lip balm to her mouth. I can smell the berry-vanilla even from a few feet away.

She blows us a kiss. I think Bess and Flora would have hugged us, but Jenny's decided a kiss blown off her finger-tips is the way to say goodbye, so they follow suit.

The kisses don't seem to reach us.

And by the time the girls are all the way down the road—without a look back at us—Mom's saying it's time to go, and Dad's checking on the rosebush in the trailer for the millionth time, and I can feel our old life forgetting us before we're even gone.

5

Made of Roses and Hills

There's a split in the car—me and Mom are chatting away, trying to ask Dad and Naomi questions, singing along with the radio, listing things we remember about Eventown: Wooden fences. Vines on the houses. Bumpless roads. Tall trees. Big smiles.

I remember the incredible farmers' market with its rows and rows of vendors selling everything from roses to raw honey to goat cheese.

"And apple cider," Naomi says. "The apple cider was my favorite."

We all take a deep inhale of remembering—it was sweet but not too sweet. It was served hot with a dollop of whipped cream on top. We all thought it was strange for there to be hot apple cider in the warm weather, but the people in town were all drinking it, so we did too. And it was a surprise delight, to be as warm inside as we were on the surface of our skin.

"Apple cider year-round," Dad says, shaking his head like the very concept is both absurd and wonderful. "What a funny little town it is."

The memory turns a little sad, like memories sometimes do, and we fall into silence.

"I need a break," Mom says when the road has been straight and empty for miles. In the last few months, Mom has often needed a break when she's in one place for too long. She needed a break in the middle of Naomi's last gymnastics competition, and she needed a break in the middle of her own birthday party. She needed a break when we all went to the movies last weekend. When she takes a break, she goes to the bathroom or to a closet or all the way outside where she can pace back and forth and stretch her arms and massage her shoulders.

We stop at the next rest stop and Mom wanders off, behind the gas station.

Dad fills up the car, and Naomi practices her favorite beam routine on one of the horizontal logs at the tops of the parking spaces. Beam is Naomi's best apparatus. She has this sort of dramatic flair to her landings—you can see the work she puts into it and the pleasure she gets from doing it well. Some people like to watch athletes who make it look easy. Naomi isn't like that. The effort is all over her face, in every part of her body, down to her scrunching toes. And when she perfects a routine, she doesn't shrug it off. She beams, she jumps up and down in the air, and her joy bursts out of her and makes everyone watching smile too. Even now, on the log, she manages a beautiful back walkover, landing on the pavement. It isn't perfect, but it's powerful and sure. She grins on her landing. She adds a few beats of dance moves—a leap and a dip and a twirl of her hands.

"I like it," I say, and I mean it. Watching my sister is fun, and since we are identical I can pretend it's me up there, all graceful and elegant and strong.

I am the brave one out in the world, but Naomi is brave when she is doing gymnastics.

She does two back handsprings on the pavement even though she's only supposed to do them when there's a mat underneath her. Right now, I swear I can see her heart pounding with adrenaline through her sweatshirt.

I wish that she could be so fearless when we're at school or at the mall or basically everywhere else. It feels lonely to have to be brave all on my own. It feels even lonelier to have to be brave *for* Naomi, who sometimes pulls me aside in the middle of the day when she's scared or nervous or sad. In those moments I try to give her a little of what I have, or remind her to treat the whole world like a gym. A place where you jump and leap and don't look down so you don't lose your balance.

"That's not how the world is," Naomi says. "In the world, I don't want everyone looking at me."

So because I'm her sister, I try to make them look at me instead.

Naomi's finally in a good mood, so I zip up my lonely feelings and try to imitate her on another one of the logs. She laughs, and I know the rest of the trip won't be as quiet as the first part.

It turns out I'm right. Naomi asks a zillion questions about Eventown School when we get back in the car, and Dad reads aloud from a pamphlet about the school. Mom seems extra-happy after her break, too, tuning the channel to some talk radio show she likes, while Dad hands out snacks from the gas station—pretzels and string cheese and bottles of chocolate milk. It's starting to feel like a real road trip, the fun kind we used to have when we drove to Washington, DC, and Niagara Falls and deep into the woods on an ill-fated camping expedition that we'll never forgive Dad for.

We stop at a diner a few hours later and order grilled

cheese sandwiches, and I think of Bess and Jenny and Flora at the mall with their pretzels and feel a pang of sadness at the way the goodbye went. Mom must notice because she orders a second plate of fries, this one with melted cheese and gravy on top, and she reminds us that when we were in Eventown there were bonfires and an enormous library we never got to explore and cute cobblestone streets.

"Remember those berries we picked?" Mom says. "Biggest blueberries I've ever seen. I wonder if Dad might be able to grow some berries on our property."

"And that beautiful restaurant in the middle of town, remember? Big skylight. Armchairs instead of dining chairs. Wasn't there even a fireplace?" Dad says. His smile makes me smile.

"There was!" Naomi says. Suddenly, we're all smiling. It feels sort of like a miracle, the four of us grinning at once for the first time in forever.

When we leave the diner, we share Eventown stories the rest of the drive, until we start seeing signs for the town. The trees get larger. The roads get windier. I think I can smell the roses and pine trees and enormous blueberries.

A sign at the border of town reads: *Welcome to Eventown, Made of Roses and Hills!* The welcome sign in Juniper says *Welcome to Juniper, Life Happens Here.*

Mom used to joke that someone very literal came up

with the Juniper town sign. "Welcome to Juniper. This is a town," she used to say, passing the sign. "Welcome to Juniper, a place where people are."

I see her light up at Eventown's sign. It's wooden with a rose carved into the place where the *o* in *Eventown* would be. There's nothing to make fun of with this sign, and for a moment it makes me sad. I'll miss Mom's joke.

Over to our left, I think I see a herd of deer. Maybe there's a special word for a group of deer, but I don't know what it is; maybe in Eventown I'll learn. We roll down the windows and listen for the sound of crickets humming.

The smell of roses is thick. It smells the way velvet feels—soft and pretty and relaxing.

The parts of me that felt sore from hours in the car now feel loose and calm.

"Home sweet new home," Dad says in his goofy Dad voice, while Mom honks the horn at the hills that shield Eventown from the rest of the world.

6

Too Much

The houses are all the same.

It's the first thing I notice when we drive up to our house, which, like every other house, is large, stone, and covered in vines. The vines are growing small purple flowers, and they wind up and down every wall.

"Everything matches," I say, and I can't decide if I love it or think it's weird. It looks beautiful but also overwhelming, to be in a town of identical houses.

"It's a quirky little town," Mom says.

"I love stone houses," Dad says.

"I love the vines!" Naomi says. So I decide to love it all too. Quirky is a good thing. We need some quirky.

In the front yard there's a huge tree with a white wooden swing hanging from it. The ropes holding the swing up are vine-covered, too, and it looks like something from a dream.

"Great work, honey," Mom says, kissing Dad right on the mouth. It's not my favorite thing, seeing Mom and Dad kiss, but right now I don't mind it. It feels like it's been a long time since I've had the opportunity to be embarrassed by their kissing and cuddling.

"Isn't it the prettiest place you've ever seen?" Dad says. His back straightens with pride, and it's been forever since I've seen that too. He looks taller. More Dad-like.

Every single house on our street has large windows and a lawn filled with rosebushes. Our old house was small, cool, all beige and tan and cream-colored. No vines growing anywhere.

"Where are everyone else's cars?" I ask. I don't see any in the driveways and I don't hear them in the distance.

"The whole town is walkable, so there's no need for cars. You know how you loved that weekend in New York City, walking everywhere? It's like that here." Mom can't stop beaming. Naomi and I both get carsick, so getting rid of the car seems like an okay idea. Better than giving up the TV, at least.

"What if we need to leave the town?" I ask, thinking of trips back to Juniper or seeing our grandparents in Virginia or taking another road trip to Montreal or Vermont.

"Oh, we can always get a car if we need it. We can rent one from the town. And it will be extra-easy for me, because I'll be working right in the main Eventown offices!"

Mom smiles every time she brings up her job with Eventown tourism. It's as if it's a brand-new thing every time the thought crosses her mind. The joy never dulls. It's nothing like the way she talked about her Juniper job.

I wish everything were like that. Other happinesses get worn out—Christmas presents that aren't so exciting come February, birthday parties that are sort of boring by the end, wonderful moments that seem sad a year later when everything has changed.

"And Dad's going to work on all the fantastic gardens around here."

"These Eventown folks love roses almost as much as I do," he says, winking in my direction. I never totally understood Dad's job, but I know he planned different public parks and designed the little garden in front of the Juniper Mall. And I know that they didn't always listen to his best ideas. And he used to complain about not getting his hands dirty in his corporate job.

I bet he'll get his hands dirty with all that Eventown gardening.

"They grow all their own vegetables too," he goes on,

"in public spaces so you kids can stay involved. I'll get to design all kinds of neat new gardens and parks."

"You'll grow and I'll cook," I say. It's a thing we used to say, and I know before it's out of my mouth that I shouldn't have said it. I can't help it, though. Words and phrases from before pop up into my head all the time, and I sort of like saying them out loud.

"That's right," Dad says with an expression that's trying to look more like a grin and less like a grimace.

"Can we go for a walk now?" Naomi asks our parents. She's good at changing the subject.

I'd hoped to spend the rest of the afternoon on that perfect swing, but Naomi's so lit up with excitement at the idea of a walk that I couldn't possibly say no. I match her smile and we do our twin thing—move very close to each other, get matching expressions on our faces, jut our hips in the same direction, and flutter our eyelashes while saying, "pleeeeeeease" in unison.

It works every time. Mom cracks a smile and Dad shakes his head like we are simply Too Much.

He used to call us Too Much with that particular smirk all the time.

He doesn't do it now, even though I'm begging him to with my eyes and the way I'm leaning my body toward him and blinking my eyelashes extra-hard.

"Dad and I need to get this car unpacked and turn it in and do some paperwork at the Welcoming Center," Mom says. "Maybe you and Naomi could explore a little on your own? What do you think, Todd?"

"Don't we have to be welcomed too?" I ask.

"Of course," Mom says. "But not today. Parents get welcomed first. You two have to check out the neighborhood for us. Let us know where all the best places are."

Dad looks a little jealous. He loves exploring. I know he's already wanting to scope out the prettiest place for a rose garden, a vegetable patch, a willow tree drooping over a field of wildflowers. "Do you think we need to do the Welcoming Center stuff right away?" he asks. Mom nods. She's always taken paperwork very seriously. She likes to keep it all in little files with color-coded Post-it notes. I bet she'll do a lot of that kind of thing at her new tourism job.

"Well, all right then," Dad says. He looks extra-hard at his rosebush, wondering, I'm sure, when he'll have a chance to replant it. Dad loves that rosebush as much as Mom loves organizing and color-coding.

Naomi's doing a little dance from foot to foot, like she has so much energy it can't be contained, and I'm trying to soak up the scent of roses and blueberries that's thick in the air.

"I want to make a cake based on the way this place

smells," I say, thinking of a blueberry cake with rose frosting and real petals and fresh berries on top.

"How delicious!" says Mom, who hasn't eaten dessert in six months. "Doesn't this place smell wonderful, Todd? We don't need our old little rosebush. This place is absolutely covered in roses."

"But this one's ours," Dad says.

"Okay, okay," Mom says with a little laugh. She bends down to kiss our cheeks and send us on our way. "You two have fun. You deserve it. And when you get back we'll have something to eat."

"Can I make dinner?" I ask. Lately I've been making a few dinners a week all by myself. I like watching my family's faces when they take a bite they find especially delicious. Part surprise, part pride.

"I think that would be just wonderful, don't you think so?" Mom says.

Everything in Eventown seems wonderful to me.

7

Friends at First Sight

We know where we want to go first. We know without having to discuss it. We know without even looking at each other.

We need ice cream. And we need it from the Eventown Ice Cream Shop, which we've talked about ever since we visited it a few years ago.

What we don't know is how to get there.

We start off down the road the way we came in, and the town is abuzz with kids on bikes and parents sitting on their front porches, pouring lemonade from crystal pitchers, tilting their faces in the direction of the sun.

Naomi does a cartwheel at the end of the road, and it's full of bounce. I've always been scared of being upside down, but I suddenly want to try one too. I lift a knee up and remind myself that Naomi and I are identical, so my body must be able to do a cartwheel if hers can. I throw my legs up and over myself, and I'm sure it looks all wrong, but it feels great, my heart leaving my body the instant I'm all the way over, then joining me again when I'm upright.

"You did it!" Naomi says.

"Sort of."

"No, you did! You really did! I never thought I'd see your legs up in the air." Naomi throws her arms around me, then hooks her elbow with mine so that we can walk in sync. "That cartwheel was a good sign," she says, whispering like she doesn't want the people of Eventown to know. "I think I'm going to love it here. It doesn't even look real, you know? It looks like a fairy tale."

I look around, and I'm seeing exactly what Naomi's seeing. A golden light instead of the harsh sun or gray clouds of Juniper. Pine trees everywhere, so tall they practically reach the sky, so tall it's hard to see the tops of them. Inviting stone houses and the stillness that comes from a town without cars.

"It's definitely a fairy tale," I say. "Like *Hansel and Gretel.*"

"But without the witch."

"Let's hope," I say. "Can't you see Little Red Riding

Hood skipping through here with her basket of food?"

"But without the wolf," Naomi says.

This was something we'd misplaced, too—our easy back-and-forth, talking about something and nothing at once. Everything becoming a game. And like that, we're walking in sync, our arms swinging in time with each other, keeping a rhythm to a song only the two of us can hear.

"You kids visiting?" a woman in a buttery-yellow dress on the next street asks. She has long black hair to her waist and brown skin and a striped straw coming out of her glass of lemonade. On her head is a big floppy straw hat, like Mom wears on vacation.

"Um, no, actually, we live here," Naomi answers.

"We moved in today," I say.

"And you're twins!" the woman says. Our twin-ness makes people happy. It always has. Sometimes it's annoying, being asked a hundred questions about it, but today we move closer to each other, shoulders touching, and don't mind the way this straw-hatted lady is looking at our matching faces. We nod. "Well, isn't that delightful," she says. "You're about the age of my daughter, Veena. I bet she'll be excited to meet you. Veena!"

A girl who looks a lot like the straw-hatted woman, but two heads smaller and with about a million necklaces around her neck, bounds out from the backyard to the front.

"Oh!" she says upon seeing us. Her smile is wide and real and impossible not to return.

"These two girls are new here," her mom says. "I'm sorry; I didn't even ask your names."

"Elodee and Naomi," I say.

"You look the same but different," Veena says instead of hello. She tilts her head and takes in Naomi's ponytail and my messy tangle of almost-curls. "I like your hair."

"I like your necklaces," I say.

"I like your house," Naomi says.

It's been a long time since we've had to make new friends, and it's a little awkward, but exciting too. Veena doesn't know anything about us. She doesn't know anything about our family or Juniper or the last year.

I take my first breath as this new Elodee, the one who isn't being boxed in by all the things everyone knew about me. I think Naomi does the same.

"We haven't had someone new our age in a long time," Veena says. Her excitement seems like it is still right below the surface of her skin, making her wiggle a little when she talks to us.

Right away, I like her. She seems odd and kind and easy to be near. *Friends at first sight*, I think.

"You're going to love it here," she says, so certain that I don't bother to ask why she thinks that or worry that she

46

could be wrong. She says it like it's a fact, so I believe it the way I believed fractions and the American Revolution and the law of gravity.

"I thought I didn't want to leave home," I say, already wanting to tell Veena all my secrets. "But I actually sort of like new places. Adventures."

"Adventures!" Veena repeats. She grins. Her eyes are bright. I can tell Naomi wishes I hadn't said so much, but Veena makes it hard to be anything but happy around her. "I think I like adventures too," she goes on. "You guys want to hang out in the backyard? It's not very adventurous, but we have a pond with a frog in it. I need help catching him."

Naomi wrinkles her nose at the idea of a slimy frog, but I'm tempted to forget all about ice cream and spend the rest of the day chasing Veena's frog.

"Actually, we were on our way to get some ice cream," Naomi says. "We visited once and had the best ice cream ever."

"But we don't remember where it was," I finish. There will be time for frogs later. Naomi needs ice cream now, so I want her to have it.

Veena claps her hands together. The charms on her necklaces jingle and jangle against each other. "Well, I can help with that," she says. "It's vanilla-rose day!"

I don't know what that means, but it sounds wonderful.

* * *

The ice cream shop is exactly as we remember it. Veena walked us here in five minutes, and I'm thinking Mom was right: no one needs a car here. Not when the best ice cream in the world is only a five-minute walk away. There are polka-dotted stools and wooden tables and a little bell that rings whenever someone enters or exits the shop. The walls are covered in yellow flowered wallpaper, and the whole place smells like a sugary garden. The people at the counter have striped shirts and jaunty chef's hats and a little glint in their eyes, like they know we're about to experience something truly special.

Today's Flavor: Vanilla-Rose, a chalkboard up front reads. And there it is, in a dozen containers behind the glass counter, soft pink ice cream with cream-colored swirls and sparkly clear sprinkles all over the top. Vanilla-rose ice cream. It looks like something made by fairies in the forest.

"One scoop each," Veena tells one of the women in striped shirts working the counter. The lady hands over three sugar cones and we eat them outside on a white bench.

It tastes even better than it looks.

It's sweet and airy and simple. The rose makes the vanilla sweeter, and the vanilla makes the rose taste a little like raspberries, but softer, smoother. And the sugary sprinkles add this tiny crunch. I can feel them sparkling in my mouth.

We swing our feet and laugh at nothing. We kick off our shoes and let the sun warm our toes. We watch Eventown residents walk in and out of the shop. They wave at Veena and she proudly introduces us as her new friends, Elodee and Naomi.

My name sounds new here. In Juniper, people said Elodee and Naomi in this awful way, like they knew everything about what being Elodee and Naomi was like. Today my name sounds mysterious. Like I could be anyone from anywhere. Like Elodee is filled with possibilities, every one of them fantastic and fun.

When we've had two cones each we head back home, and Veena chatters on the whole way. She doesn't ask us anything about where we came from or why we moved here. And without TV or movies or the internet, we can't talk about any of the things we talked to Bess and Flora and Jenny about. Instead we talk about favorite flowers and colors and cookies. She tells us a dozen of her favorite things in Eventown—the ice cream, of course, the library, the school, the park, the bonfires, the new butterfly house, the blueberries, the market, the sunsets.

By the time we're back at Veena's house, Naomi and I are so excited about starting school that we almost wish we could begin tonight.

"I'll walk with you to school tomorrow!" Veena calls, waving goodbye with her mother, who's given us paper cups of lemonade for the walk home. The lemonade is flavored with something special—mint or basil, I think—and it tastes like a perfect summer day.

When we finally get back to our house, I go right for the kitchen. It was nice exploring the town, but I want to know what size the oven is and how high the counters are, and I want to plan how I will organize myself when I'm cooking and baking in here.

It's better than I could have imagined. The counters are shiny and there's a full set of copper pots and pans hanging from the ceiling that the previous owner must have left behind. The stove looks old-fashioned—black and large and welcoming. It looks like a kitchen from a magazine.

I step back to admire it all. "Wow. Where'd this all come from?"

"Eventown tourism sets it up for new families," Mom says. "That will be part of my job once a year too. Pretty special, right?"

I'm too impressed to even nod.

Mom and Dad hold hands, watching me take it in. They grin at each other, at me, at the way the copper pots and pans glint as the sun sets.

"It gets better," Mom says, barely able to contain herself. It's hard to believe it could get better than this. She hands me a small wooden box. "They left this for you."

I open the box. Inside are dozens and dozens of recipes, maybe hundreds, written on butter-stained index cards. The writing is tidy and cursive. The recipes look well-loved and each recipe sounds amazing—cookies and pies and elaborate gourmet meals. There are instructions for Eventown's Favorite Bacon and Eggs, Your New Favorite Turkey Club, Perfect Chicken Noodle Soup.

"We might have told them a little about you loving cooking," Mom says. "The town put it together for you." She has happy tears in her eyes. For months, all the tears in her eyes have been sad ones. I give her a huge hug. Dad too. Naomi leaps into the fold and pulls out a recipe for fried chicken.

"Dinner!" she exclaims.

"Looks delicious," Mom says, pulling away from the group hug. "Why don't you come with me and we'll pick up all the ingredients?" Naomi usually hates grocery shopping with Mom, but I know she wants to see more of the town, so she practically sprints out the door.

"Perfect," Dad says. "Leaves Elodee and me a little time to work on the garden."

I roll my eyes, but I don't actually mind. The sun is a cozy kind of warm and the garden is beautiful already. I help Dad put the rosebush in its new spot. There are rosebushes everywhere, but he's right: it's nice to have one that's just ours.

"I'll help you watch over it," I say, because he looks

sort of lonely, staring at it.

I've said the right thing and unlocked Dad's big, goofy, not-so-lonely-after-all smile. "It'll be our rosebush," Dad says. "Our project together. Taking care of this tiny bit of Juniper. We're in it together, okay?"

I say okay, even though it feels sort of wrong, because the rosebush was never mine. But it makes Dad happy to hear me say okay and to see me grab the watering can and give it a gentle sprinkling.

"My little gardener," Dad says, even though I've never been very good at gardening at all.

When Mom and Naomi get back from grocery shopping, I get right to work, and the cooking comes easily. The instructions are clear, and following the recipe feels like a dance with the kitchen. The result is incredible. The chicken is golden brown, crispy on the outside and buttery on the inside. The slaw on the side is a little salty and a little vinegar-y and reminds me of Fourth of July picnics. I've never made anything this delicious. I've made things that are fun and messy and bizarre. But the recipes I invented in our old kitchen back in Juniper were never like this.

As we eat, I forget every other bite of chicken I've ever taken. I forget every other meal I've ever had. I forget every moment, but this one, right here, in Eventown.

8

The Long Way

Veena's agreed to walk us to school, and Mom and Dad keep saying we need to *jump right in* and *find our routine*, so we are doing exactly that. The first day of third grade in Juniper, Naomi was so scared she cried on the bus, and I spent the whole time rubbing her back. The first day of fourth grade in Juniper, Naomi threw up in the bathroom before the first bell rang and I promised not to tell anyone. Our first day of sixth grade in Juniper, even I was nervous. Mom said we could stay home. We weren't ready. We slipped into sixth grade a week later, and everyone pretended we'd been there all along.

But my first day of sixth grade in Eventown, six months after my first day of sixth grade in Juniper, feels fine. Naomi seems so calm it might as well not be the first day of school at all. She's dressed up as usual, in a pink dress with her hair in a high, bouncy ponytail. I put on a gray dress that I never wore in Juniper but that feels good here. I pair it with sneakers and keep my almost-red hair down and messy around my shoulders. People have trouble telling us apart, but I don't really know why. Naomi is all smoothed out and fancy. I usually look a little messy even when I'm trying really hard to be neat.

Mom starts to brush my hair for me, but she stops herself. She knows I'll just shake her off. I like my hair like this. I like to not look exactly like my twin.

For breakfast I make French toast from a recipe in the box. It is cinnamon-y and thick and it doesn't go all soggy under the maple syrup. I can't believe the taste. Not too eggy. Not too sweet. Perfect, again.

"It's a good sign for your first day," Mom says, as sure as I've heard her about anything.

Dad comes in from outside all covered in dirt and smiles.

"Roses just love it here!" he says. "Look out the window, Elodee. Our rosebush is so happy in that Eventown soil."

Naomi tilts her head at Dad calling the rosebush *ours*, and I shrug in return.

I look out the window as instructed, and he's right. The rosebush almost seems like it's tilting itself toward the sun. I swear it's redder than before.

"We're a good team," Dad says, and again Naomi's face scrunches with confusion. I'm the chef of the family, not the gardener, and Dad has kept all his talk of soil and sun and watering cans to himself since last summer. It's funny to have it all out in the open again.

But nice too. He takes a big inhale and grins. "And what do I smell here? French toast? Smells spectacular. Did my favorite chef make that?"

I nod.

"How lucky am I?" he says, and serves himself some breakfast. He finally sees Naomi, who I think was feeling a little left out. "Omi, you look beautiful. All grown up." Naomi blushes—at the compliment but also at the nickname. Another thing that's gone unused for many months.

We exchange more glances, but Dad's good mood is infectious, and soon Mom and Dad are ushering us out the door with kisses and waves and have-a-good-days. The sun hasn't quite finished rising, and the sky is rosy from almost-daylight, and Veena's right outside waiting for us. March is warmer here than it was in Juniper, and I don't miss my big down jacket or the way my ears feel itchy under a wool hat.

Veena introduces herself to Mom and Dad, who look relieved we have a friend already, and she tells us everyone is excited for us to come to school.

I like how straight her back is and how she looks a little dreamy-eyed. She has even more necklaces around her neck today. Some look like fake pearls and some look like real gold and one looks really heavy—a metal rose hanging from a leather cord. I want to touch it, but we're not friends like that. Not yet, at least.

Veena takes us the long way to school. "You'll like it," she says. "I always go the long way. Everyone does."

I laugh because it sounds like a joke, but Veena doesn't laugh.

Naomi looks puzzled. We dip into the woods, away from the main road. Veena's voice drops to a whisper even though there's no one around to hear us talk. "Don't you think the long way somewhere is almost always prettier than the short way?"

"I've never thought about it before," I say.

"I guess it is," Naomi says. In Juniper there's traffic in every direction from everyone trying to get somewhere else the quickest way possible. And then it ends up taking extra long to get somewhere because of how hard we're all trying to get there quickly. It makes me laugh a little, thinking about it.

"This is the best part," Veena says. We've come to a bridge suspended over a miniature waterfall. Somehow, in the middle of the woods, rosebushes still grow wild, the roses fully bloomed and reaching toward the now-almost-fully-risen sun. It feels like the sunrise is longer and prettier

56

here in Eventown. Like everything, even the way the sun moves across the sky, is better here.

It's so beautiful, I trip and stumble over the bridge. Dewdrops cling to the flowers and glint in the sun. Butterflies whisper around our shoulders, over the tops of our heads, and the pine trees are so tall I can't see the tops of them; I can't see where the woods end.

Which is great, because I don't want it to end.

"This is how you get to school every day?" Naomi asks, staring at the waterfall. "Like, you don't have a bus?"

"Oh, like one of those yellow ones?" Veena asks.

Naomi and I nod in unison.

"I've heard about those, but we've never had them here. They can fit tons of people, and you're all stuck in there until you get to school? Right?"

I nod. "There's gum on the seats," I say.

"Everyone pays a lot of attention to where you sit, and if you sit in the wrong place, people think you're not cool," Naomi says.

"Sometimes you feel sick on the bus," I add.

"Oh, and it's sort of smelly."

"And loud!"

"Yes! Really loud! And then when it's too loud, the bus driver yells at us or even pulls the bus over until we're all quiet."

Veena is stunned. She sits on the bridge, right in the middle, her legs dangling off the thing, trying to process.

"Why would they do that to you?" she asks.

"It's just—it makes it easier?" Naomi looks to me, like I know the answers to why we've done everything the way we've always done it.

"It doesn't sound easy," Veena says. She gets up and runs to the other side of the bridge. She doesn't seem to mind the way it swings and buckles from her footsteps. She isn't scared, and, I realize, neither am I.

I could walk across the bridge, and maybe that's what I would have done back home, but I'm not in Juniper anymore.

So I skip.

9

Where We Used to Live

Three people compliment me on my dress before we're even all the way inside the school. They like my dress and Naomi's shoes and the fact that we look exactly the same.

A boy with brown skin and huge glasses opens up his lunch box and offers us the world's biggest peanut butter cookie. A girl with straight hair and a high voice gives us big hugs. "I'm so happy you're here!" she says.

"Their mom's going to work for the tourism office," Veena tells everyone we meet. "And their dad is going to be in charge of a bunch of the gardens. And they're twins." I love that this is all Veena knows about us, and that she seems so proud to show us off. The girl with the straight

59

hair and high voice—her name is Betsy—is the only one who I don't immediately like. She reminds me a little of Jenny from back home, and she's almost too sweet. She has a lot of questions about Mom's new job and the vacation we took here a few years ago.

"I always wonder how people find us," she says. "We don't have that many people vacationing here, but when we do I'm always really curious why they came here and not, like, Disney World or something."

Something about the way she says the word *curious* makes me squeeze my hands into fists at my sides. When Naomi's upset she gets very quiet and cries late at night when she thinks I'm not awake. But when I'm upset, especially lately, I get angry. And Betsy's voice is making me angry. And being angry makes me even angrier.

"Well, I'm sure I'll be able to answer that soon. Since my mom's job will be getting more visitors here," I say. I'm not sure if this is exactly true, but it seems like something Eventown tourism would be in charge of. And she said she'd be in charge of some "exciting new initiatives," which sounds like fancy-talk for making tourism better.

"I didn't know we wanted more visitors," Betsy says.

"I do!" Veena interrupts, and maybe I'm the only one hearing something less than nice in Betsy's voice. Naomi says I'm too sensitive sometimes, that I notice things that aren't really there. "There was a family visiting here last month and one of the boys was *so* cute. And remember the really nice couple over the summer, Betsy? They taught us how to make friendship bracelets. They said their vacation was just what they needed."

"What did they need?" I ask. I remember Mom and Dad saying something similar about our vacation here. I remember them saying it helped our family. I think it just put us in a good, relaxed mood. I could see Eventown doing that for pretty much everyone.

Veena shrugs. "I'll teach you guys how to make friend-ship bracelets, if you don't already know," she says, as if that's the most important part of the story. And maybe it is, because Bess and Jenny learned how to make friendship bracelets at camp last summer and never showed us how.

Betsy locks her arm with Naomi, and Veena does the same to me. Naomi looks over at me and beams. She loves belonging.

"I've been hoping someone new would come," Veena whispers to me.

"You have?" We never liked new kids in Juniper. Some-times they got so much attention from everyone that we felt jealous, and sometimes they were shy and teachers scolded us for not being more welcoming.

"I want to show you everything. Everyone's so nice here,

but I've never had a best, best friend, you know?" Veena's talking so fast I have trouble keeping up. I can't be sure, but it sounds like she asked me to be her best friend. "I mean, everyone's like best friends here," Veena says quickly, like she's said something wrong. "We're all best friends, but I always want *new* best friends. That's what I meant. My mom had a best friend a long time ago. She says someday she'll tell me all her stories about it." Veena plays with one of her necklaces. Red beads with a little broken heart at the end. It looks like the kind of necklace that has a pair, that's meant to be locked with someone else's necklace.

A best friend's.

I have a lot of questions, but I nod like I understand because I don't want to interrupt the warm, glowy feeling I'm getting being around all these people. It feels like the beautiful sunset we watched last night is inside me, like it lasted so long that I swallowed it whole and I get to carry it around so I can feel golden-pink and toasty.

The school is so small that I'm pretty sure I've met every single kid by lunchtime. In the fifth grade, there's only twelve of us, so it's easy to learn their names and I can almost feel like I'm not a new kid at all.

In math class we play Monopoly and in science we do a bunch of experiments that feel more like magic than schoolwork. In History of Eventown we all draw pictures of the town, so it's sort of more like art class. I've never had so much fun in school. The kids are friendly and nice and no one has a clique. The teachers all have big, cheery smiles and not a single chair has an annoying squeak. No one's written mean things about anyone else on the desks or in the bathroom stalls. I can hear birds outside the window, singing little songs to each other. There are delicious sandwiches at lunch, absolutely smothered in melted cheese that never goes cold and rubbery. I could eat a dozen of them.

Kids speak in hushed, happy tones in the cafeteria, but no one seems to mind that I don't sound that way. Back in Juniper, Jon called my voice loud and annoying, and he said Naomi sounded like a tiny little mouse. But no one here seems to mind the way we sound.

We're fine, just as we are. Good, even.

"I like this school," Naomi says, and I nod in agreement.

We feel so far away from Juniper, I could almost forget all about shoving Jenny and the way everyone looked at me. I decide not to be that kind of person here. I decide to be calm and nice and fun, like Veena. Like Naomi's probably always wanted me to be.

"We moved here right before I was born," Veena says. "So I don't know about other places people live, but it's pretty much perfect here."

"It *is*," Betsy says. "My moms and I moved here five years ago, and it's so much better than—than the place we were."

"Where were you before?" I ask. I'm having trouble imagining Betsy outside of Eventown.

"Ugh, the worst place ever," Betsy says. "You wouldn't know it. It was so ugly I don't even like to think about it."

"Maybe I'll stop thinking about Juniper," Naomi says, like not talking about our old home is the best idea anyone's ever had. I can already tell Naomi wants to be just like Betsy. There's always someone Naomi wants to be just like. Back home it was Bess.

But she's right. It might be okay to stop thinking so much about Juniper. Maybe we can forget about the worst parts. Like the smell of the mall—fake cinnamon sugar and faker fruity body spray. Our old school with its ugly brown floors and mushy chicken tenders and ringing bell that was so loud it would make me leap in my chair whenever it rang. The dog next door who used to bark early every morning or the enormous cars honking their horns and playing bad music too loud out their windows.

We can forget it all, if we want.

"Yeah," I say. "We don't need to talk about where we used to live. We don't live there anymore."

"Good," Betsy says, smiling.

"Good," Naomi says.

And it is.

10

The Same Kind of Brave

For the next three days, on the walk to school, Veena tells us what to expect from the day. On Tuesday there's gym. We play capture the flag, and I feel like I run faster in Eventown, like I'm lighter on my feet.

On Wednesday we have a math test, and I'm pretty sure I ace it. Somehow the way our teacher here in Eventown explains fractions is simpler than the way our Juniper teacher did. In Juniper our teacher used to just talk more loudly and more slowly when I asked him to explain something. Here Ms. Applebet has a billion ways to explain everything, and she doesn't stop until we get it. She makes up silly songs about numbers and uses five different colors of marker to write things on the whiteboard.

On Thursday Veena announces we have music class.

"Oh," I say. Naomi and I don't like music class, but I don't want to tell Veena that. Everything's been so good and easy, I don't want to ruin it with our Juniper worries.

"Music?" Naomi asks, with a pained look on her face. I can tell she doesn't want to get into it either, but she also really, really doesn't want to go to music class. With Naomi so nervous, I know I have to take care of her. I rub her back.

"We'll be okay," I say. "If the teacher's mean, I'll be mean right back." Naomi gives a half smile. She doesn't try to make me feel any better, though. I wish she would.

"Yeah!" Veena says, skipping as always. "Music! With Mr. Fountain. It's my favorite." Over the last few days, Veena has said approximately twenty-five different things are her favorite. Then she always changes her mind right away, to have another favorite. Naomi and I give each other a sneaky-smirky glance and wait for her to do it now. She does, of course. "Well. Some days gym is my favorite. And some days English is. And some days math is. But music is my favorite a lot of days."

"We don't like music class," I say. I check in with Naomi again and wait for her to say more, to back me up. But she just twirls a strand of hair that's come loose from her ponytail and stares at the ground. I try to stand up straighter, to be even braver.

In Juniper, music was the thing I hated the most. Our teacher was Mrs. Jones, and she never smiled. She told us music took discipline and if we wanted to be musicians we better stop fooling around and start acting our age. She never let us play anything fun. She rarely even let us play or sing songs at all, mostly just scales.

"You'll like it here," Veena says.

When we get to music class, Mr. Fountain asks what my favorite instrument is. No one's ever cared before what instrument I might like, but I know the answer anyway.

"The triangle," I say.

"Perfect," Mr. Fountain says. "I've got a triangle with your name on it." He hands me the silver triangle and the tiny wand that goes with it. My heart soars. In Juniper, I never got to be on triangle. Mrs. Jones always gave triangle to the popular girls, the pretty girls, the girls with delicate fingers and sweet smiles. I was usually on xylophone. On my worst days she gave me a wooden block and a drumstick and tried to convince me that was a valid musical instrument.

If I were to make a Mrs. Jones cake, it would be a coffee cake with angry, spicy frosting and a lot of crunchy nuts on top.

But I'd rather think of cakes to make for everyone in Eventown. A Veena cake would be lemon and lime with an airy whipped cream and serious, rich dark chocolate in the center. A Betsy cake would be overwhelmed with cherry syrup and white chocolate and the thickest buttercream frosting anyone's ever tasted. A little too sweet.

"How about you, Naomi?" Mr. Fountain asks after I've shown off my natural triangle skills with a few brilliant *ting-ting-tings!*

"Oh. Well. I guess anything is fine," she says. Naomi only likes people to notice her when she's being Gymnast Naomi. I think she'd be happiest just humming along in music class.

Mr. Fountain squints. He considers Naomi. "Let me see your hands," he says. She shows him. They are calloused from the bars and so strong. "Good. Now clap them together. Hard." Naomi does. She starts quietly but gets louder. She's next to me, so the sound is loud in my ears, but I nod encouragement at her.

"Now here's the big question," Mr. Fountain says. His voice is very serious. "Are you brave?"

Naomi squirms, so I answer for her. "The bravest," I say, because Naomi tried a cartwheel on the beam before she'd even mastered it on the floor and she pulled up onto the bars without a spotter when everyone else on her team needed their coach beside them, holding their shoulders as they swung up high. Naomi doesn't think she's as brave as me, but that's only because she's a different kind of brave. All the different kinds of brave were explained to me once, and sometimes I wish Naomi and I were the same kind of brave, but we're not.

Sometimes it's extra-lonely to look so much alike but be so different inside.

It's a thought I keep to myself, even though there was a time when I would have felt comfortable sharing it with someone. I keep a lot more to myself these days.

I grip my instrument and tell my brain and my heart to quiet down and enjoy the triangle.

"If you're brave, I know exactly what instrument to give you," Mr. Fountain says. "No one leaves my class without falling in love with music. It's okay to come in and not like it. But we'll find what you're meant to do in here."

He has a bushy beard, which he scratches. He moves to the back of the classroom, where there are boxes and boxes of abandoned instruments. Maybe he'll find Naomi a flute or a violin. Maybe there's another triangle—gold instead of silver, big instead of small. Maybe there's a harmonica. I think Naomi could play the harmonica.

But instead of a harmonica or a flute, Mr. Fountain comes back with the very last thing I'd expect.

Cymbals.

Not small, cute, Naomi-sized cymbals.

Big, brass cymbals, so big she'll get out of breath from one single crash.

I am sure Naomi will hate them. Naomi is quieter than me. I have to beg her to let me bring friends to her gymnastics meets. On our birthdays she lets me blow out the candles; she likes that all the attention doesn't have to be on her. Even when we were little, she always wanted to be the hider in hide-and-go-seek. She'd find the best place to hide, and when I'd find her, she'd look disappointed that she didn't have more time to be invisible.

"I think you're going to like these," Mr. Fountain says. He huffs and puffs a little, carrying the enormous things to the front of the room.

I laugh. "I don't think so!" I say.

I expect Naomi to agree. But when I look at her she's all wide-eyed and smiling.

"Actually," she says, "those look great."

"Really?" I ask. "Those things are, like, the opposite of the triangle."

"So?"

"So, I thought we both liked the triangle." I hang on to the things Naomi and I feel the same way about, because the ways that we're different make me sad. We like the crunch of leaves when they turn orange and fall to the ground and reading books after lights out and the place in the Juniper

Mall with a jukebox. We've always had the same friends and the same way of holding a pencil and a paintbrush and the same fear of the bottom of the ocean. And, I thought, we both always wanted to play the triangle.

"That's your thing," Naomi says, like it's nothing to strip away one of the things we share. "I didn't think I wanted to play anything. But these—these look cool."

"Try them!" Mr. Fountain says. His eyebrows are as bushy as his beard, and they spike and wiggle.

Naomi takes one cymbal in each hand. She swings her arms out to the side, and with a great exhale of breath, brings them together.

Crash!

It's the loudest noise in the world, and it makes me want to cover my ears, but Naomi is beaming.

"Yes," she says. "Perfect."

Mr. Fountain nods and his bushy eyebrows bounce around.

I don't think Naomi would have played cymbals in Juniper. And it makes me wonder what else might be different here in Eventown.

Betsy's on xylophone and Veena gets to play a few chords on the class piano and all the kids in class look happy with the instrument they've been assigned. There's a rustling of papers, and Mr. Fountain puts the sheet music in front of me and Naomi. "The Eventown Anthem," it reads.

"Oh," I say. "We don't know how to read music. We never learned at our old school."

"You'll catch up," Mr. Fountain says, as sure as ice cream is delicious and Saturdays are the best day of any week.

The other kids start playing, and the song is familiar somehow, even though I can't remember ever hearing it before. My hand and my heart seem to know when to ding my triangle. It's a little hard to hear the fairy sound over everyone else's instruments, but when the noise hits my ears, it's the most beautiful sound in the world.

I never want to stop.

I look over at Naomi, and I can tell she feels the same way. She gets this look on her face the moment before she crashes the cymbals together. Like she has a sneaky secret. Like she's breaking the rules. Like she has something no one else can understand.

Even me.

I try to focus on the music, and it's pretty easy to do. We sound good. We sound great, actually. "The Eventown Anthem" is cheery and melodic. I can't help but bounce my shoulders along with the beat. Naomi smiles at the recorder trills coming from the wind section and the high notes Betsy hits over and over on her xylophone.

I never knew someone could be so happy playing a xylophone.

"This is perfect," I mouth to Naomi across the room. She has shiny eyes and bouncing shoulders just like mine. She nods back at me.

In Juniper, nothing was ever perfect. Especially not lately. I didn't think anything would ever be perfect again.

But here in Eventown, perfect seems possible.

11
A Blue That Wants to Be Purple

The next morning, Mom's got on hiking boots and jeans and a flannel shirt that I'm pretty sure belongs to Dad.

"Surprise!" Mom says. The word stops me. There's only ever been one person in the family who liked surprising me and Naomi, and it wasn't ever Mom. I don't like surprises anymore. They give me a bad taste in my mouth. They feel scary now. "Your class is going on a blueberry-picking field trip and I'm coming along!"

Veena told us about blueberry-picking day, and no one loves blueberries as much as Mom. So it makes sense that she would want to come.

Still, she should know I don't like surprises. A little

flutter of anger hums in my chest. I want to shake it off. Back in Juniper, the school counselor said some people feel anger easily and some people feel sadness easily and some people feel fear easily. I told her I want to be a person who feels happiness easily. She smiled a funny smile. And that smile made me feel angry too.

I don't want to be angry in Eventown, so I take a deep breath and try to find another feeling somewhere in me.

For once, another feeling is there.

Wonder.

There's a lot of wonder here—delicious ice cream and waterfalls on the walk to school and so many flowers they make my head spin.

I fill myself with wonder now. It feels a little like sparkle and a little like excitement, and a little like the last dive down on a roller coaster and a little like the first five seconds after a dream.

It's better than anger, that's for sure.

"Sounds fun," I say. I'm still a little angry, underneath the hope, but I tell it to be quiet.

Mom beams. "You can make a blueberry pie later, Elodee! I saw a recipe in the box. And one for blueberry pancakes too." Mom rubs my back, like she might rub the anger right off me. And maybe she can.

* * *

All twelve Eventown fifth graders are waiting outside the schoolhouse for us when we arrive. They have baskets hooked over their arms, and I look around for a field trip bus before remembering there are no cars or buses here.

Betsy's brought baskets for Naomi and Mom and me, and Veena's brought us big straw hats that match hers and the one her mom was wearing the other day.

"Blueberry-picking hats," she says before placing them on our heads. Mine's a little too floppy and Naomi's is a little too wide, but I can tell from Naomi's grin that she's thrilled to be matching with our new friends. So I decide to like the hats too.

The little sparks of Elodee-anger I felt earlier today are gone. Mom, Naomi, and I stopped at the waterfall on our way here and tried to reach out and touch the cool spray; we fell in love with a certain shade of pink taking over the sky; and Mom promised we could go to the monthly bonfire over the weekend. We remembered the smell of the fire and the endless supply of roasted marshmallows.

"We loved that bonfire," Mom said. "And now we can go every month." She's excited all the time now, from not being able to keep up with every wonderful bit of our new life.

It's impossible to be angry, after all that.

The walk to the lowest point on the Eventown Hills

is quick, and the second we're at the grassy base, we come across an enormous blueberry patch.

"Pick gently," Betsy says.

"But if you don't, you get to lick all the juices off your fingers," Veena says. Betsy rolls her eyes, and I bet Betsy has never picked a blueberry too hard in her life. I'd rather be more like Veena.

But I know Naomi wants to do everything perfectly, even blueberry picking. And she probably wants me to try to do it perfectly too. I'm not going to, though.

"You guys pick the first ones," Veena says. I look for Mom, but she's chatting with a few of the teachers. She's leaning against a pine tree, not worrying about sap getting in her hair or what to say next. She looks entirely unworried, and I wonder if I've ever seen Mom without a single worry.

Naomi grins at me. "How many do we need for you to make a pie, muffins, and pancakes?"

"Um, a lot," I say. "Maybe four hundred?"

"Then we've got some work to do."

"You bake?" Veena asks. "What's your favorite thing to bake?"

"It's different every day," I say. I imagine savory cakes or cupcakes with peanut butter frosting or goat cheese in the center. Fruit brownies made from strawberry jam. Caramel bread with slices of apple on top. Basil-and-orange popsicles. Cookie-dough scones. I want to bake them all.

Naomi nudges me. "Earth to Elodee!"

I grin. "Sorry." Naomi just laughs. She's used to my food daydreams by now. "I was thinking about what might be the best thing to bake."

"Probably something from the recipe box!" Naomi says. It's not what I want her to say. And when Naomi says the wrong thing, it's worse than when someone else does. When I was littler I thought a twin was a promise to always have someone understand you.

But lately I have to realize, over and over, that that's not really true.

"Don't forget about the berries," Naomi says, reaching her hand out to the bush in front of us. I do the same, and we each pick a berry. They're enormous, larger than two or three regular blueberries put together. The color is deep and shiny—a blue that wants to be purple. Naomi raises her eyebrows. I raise mine right back. We pop the first pick in our mouths instead of into our baskets, and the taste is unbearably beautiful. Sweet and tangy and so sure of itself. It tastes like we are eating the color itself, not the fruit. We are eating blue-purple, and it tastes so good I almost don't want to turn it into pies and muffins and pancakes. I almost don't want to pick blueberries at all anymore. I wouldn't mind sitting in a patch of sun and devouring them by the handful until my mouth is blue and my legs are lazy.

"It's like the book," I say.

"What book?" Naomi asks. She's having the same experience as I am. Her jaw is relaxed; her eyes are hungry for more.

"That picture book we used to have. About blueberries. About how amazing it is to pick them."

Naomi leans her head back and closes her eyes. Normally, she'd remember every title in our huge bookcase back home.

"Did we bring that book with us? About the blueberries?" I call to Mom, still leaning against the tree, laughing with the teachers.

"Hm? I don't know, sweetie," she calls back. She sneaks a berry into her mouth and smiles like it's a secret we share.

"What was it called? The blueberry one, Mom." Mom walks over to me and shrugs and tucks some hair behind my ear.

"Oh, who knows?" Mom says. "You two had so many books." She takes a blueberry out of my basket, grinning at the taste when she puts it in her mouth. I notice the past tense. I remember seeing shelves of books left behind, but I assumed we'd brought along our favorites. We've always had a house filled with books. So many that we can forget the titles of even our most favorite ones.

Now I have a sneaking suspicion we might not have packed any of them. Not even the ones we loved so hard the binding is broken and the pages are stained. I suddenly miss every single one of them.

"*Blueberries for Sal*," Naomi says at last.

"Yes!" I say. "Do you know that one, Veena?"

"I only care about blueberries for Veena!" Veena says.

"Maybe we can pick it up from the library later," I say, turning back to the bushes. I pick another berry, almost eat it, but put it in my basket instead. Then another. Each one is warm in my hand and delicate, about to burst.

"Oh, the library! I want to go to the library!" Naomi says. We passed it the other day and it was every bit as beautiful as we'd remembered—a huge stone building with skylights and towering bookcases and potted flowers in every window. We even caught sight of an enormous fireplace inside, with big overstuffed chairs circled around it.

"It's a special place," Mom says. "I'm learning all about it at work. One of the best attractions here in Eventown. It's under renovation now, but as soon as it's open we'll go."

We nod and try to think of other books we'll check out of the library while we return to our berry picking.

"You guys are so funny," Betsy says. "You're, like, obsessed with books."

"We love stories," I say.

Naomi's quiet. If Betsy doesn't like books and stories, Naomi won't want to either.

"You'll love the Welcoming Center if you like stories," Veena says.

"They have books there?" I ask.

"They have all the stories," Betsy answers. Veena is quiet. Naomi and I look to Mom, a few feet away.

"Are we going to the Welcoming Center soon?" I ask. "It might be even better than the library!"

"Soon," Mom says. "I promise."

I hope it has the story of Eventown and why it's so different from other places, because I have so many questions. I want to know the story of Veena and of Betsy and of Mr. Fountain and of blueberry hills and why there are perfect sunsets. It's hard to know much of anything if you don't know all the stories of a place and the people in it.

When our baskets are full, Veena and Betsy have made their way back over to us, and Mom kisses our cheeks in front of everyone and we're not even embarrassed about it.

"You taste like blueberries," Mom says.

"The air tastes like blueberries," Naomi says, and it's so true it makes me smile.

It's the best day of school I've ever had.

I feel guilty for the thought. Maybe I'm not supposed to have a great day of school. Not yet.

I tell the guilt to go away, and try to be like Naomi, like Betsy, like Veena.

The taste of blueberries is wild and bright in my mouth, and I tell myself that nothing else matters.

12

The Taste of Green

I make blueberry pancakes Saturday morning, of course.
They are fluffy and thick. A little like cake and a little like
a biscuit and a little like something else entirely, something
new.

I wonder if I could make blueberry pancake bread.
Or blueberry-chocolate-applesauce cupcakes. I imagine
bringing boxes of them to school and being celebrated as the
best baker in Eventown. The idea makes my toes scrunch
up with excitement.

Dad's already gone by the time we're up and eating
breakfast, which seems impossible because the sun is still
rising in the sky. Dad didn't used to be an early riser, but

I've noticed that in the week that we've been here, he's up early. I take my pancake out to the rosebush he has been calling "our rosebush." It fits right in with the Eventown rosebushes. The petals look like velvet, the blooms are bigger than they ever were at home, and somehow even the plant looks as happy as the rest of us.

I pick up the watering can that Dad keeps in the garden and water the rosebush.

"Hey, another gardener!" someone calls from next door. Mom's spent time with the neighbors, Maggie and Victor, and I know they have a son in high school, but I haven't seen him before.

"My dad's the gardener," I say. "I'm just . . . I'm helping."

"You look like a professional to me," the boy says. He has long legs and a goofy smile, and right away I want to be his friend.

I giggle. It's a giggle I haven't heard myself have for a long time. "I'm Elodee," I say, "the professional rose-waterer."

"Baxter," the boy says. "I'm still only an amateur, sadly."

I giggle again. If Naomi saw, she'd say I have a crush, but I don't.

"It's all in the wrist," I say, and demonstrate by watering the grass that is so green it doesn't need a drop more of water.

"Ohhhh," Baxter says. "I thought it was in the legs." He jumps up and down while watering one of his rosebushes.

My giggles keep coming out, a whole waterfall of them. It feels great, then, all of a sudden, it hurts.

Naomi would hate the hurting. I think it's okay, sometimes, for a memory to hurt.

"You have a lot to learn," I say, trying to stay light and giggly, but my heart is aching inside and it feels like it must be visible on my face and even in my elbows, my neck, my shins. "I gotta go back inside."

"More pointers tomorrow?" Baxter asks. I can tell from the way it comes out all natural that he's like this with everyone, not just me, and that hurts a little too.

"Sure," I say, but I'm not sure I'll come out and water the rosebush at this time tomorrow. It's hard to tell if I want to see more of Baxter or less. It seems like I should be able to know what I want, and the not-knowing makes my shoulders tense and my neck tighten and my face get hot with anger. I head back inside, and I want to stomp my feet and punch a pillow, but Mom and Naomi are still happy with their pancakes and the morning sun and I don't want to feel bad all alone.

I get another pancake. It helps, but only a little.

"Can we visit Dad at work?" I ask. "I want to bring him some of these pancakes. He likes them cold, remember?"

Dad is designing a garden in the center of town, and I want to see what he's come up with. Plus, I just want to be near him after talking to Baxter. I want the whole family together.

"That sounds wonderful," Mom says. She serves herself two more pancakes, drowning them in syrup.

"And then the library?" Naomi asks.

Mom doesn't respond as quickly. "Well, it's a little different from our library back home," she says. "It's still closed right now. But the good news is there are dozens of wonderful places for us to spend the day. I don't think you girls have seen the biggest waterfall in town yet, have you? It's on the top of the tallest Eventown hill. Or there's a butterfly house that Veena's mother, Ms. Butra, works at. It's a new addition to the town. Quite an experience, from what I've heard."

In Juniper, there was a lot of silence. Hours of it. Days of it, sometimes. Sometimes when I got to school my voice would be scratchy from all the not-talking I was doing. So it's a shock to hear Mom so excited about a simple weekend activity.

I'm still catching up with all the things Mom's saying, but she keeps going. "And maybe after the butterflies, we could go look at the place where we're thinking of holding the first Eventown Carnival. It's my new initiative. A way to include tourists in the town fun, but also make tourist season a little more contained. So much to show you girls!"

"Contained?" I ask.

"The town wants a set tourist season every year. Since the weather is always so nice, usually there are visitors year-round. We're hoping the Eventown Carnival will bring the visitors all at the same time. Make things simpler."

"How?" I like talking about Mom's and Dad's jobs here in Eventown. I like the way they both get excited about their work and how when they're talking about it they don't seem worried about things like my tangled-up hair or my bedtime or my math test.

I like how Mom's eyes shine. I like how Dad has to pull up photos of different flowers to show me, even though they all look sort of the same to me.

Mom doesn't answer this question, though. "Such a curious cat, my Elodee," she says instead. "I think you'll understand so much more about the town after we take you girls to the Welcoming Center. You may have a lot of questions right now, but I think you'll find things are actually really simple here."

"Good," Naomi says. She doesn't like big crowds or complicated friendships or asking too many questions or my most intricate recipes. She likes cheese pizza and a perfect cartwheel and taking the same walk to school every morning with Veena. Simple.

"How about we go to the butterfly house today, okay?"

Mom says. "Ms. Butra can't stop raving about it. It's one of the first new attractions in years and years here. It's a new Eventown tradition. And this town loves traditions."

I wait for Naomi to squirm or roll her eyes or say no. I wait for Dad to appear and sigh and say he's too tired. But that doesn't happen. Naomi says it sounds great, and I agree, and I bet even Dad would think the butterfly house here in Eventown sounds like exactly the right thing to do today.

The center of town is bustling. Friendly faces are everywhere, but I just want to see my dad's smile. There's a big yard in the center of town where Dad will be designing his first garden. For now, though, it's mostly just green with a few patches of fruits and vegetables and herbs growing in the center. I'm curious right away about what delicious fresh things might be growing here.

Kids from school wave to Naomi and me, and when we say we're going to see the butterflies, they get every bit as excited as Mom was when she talked about them.

"I've gone every week since it opened," Charlie says. "And I'm going to go every week until forever." I laugh a little, but Charlie is serious about the butterfly house, so I turn serious too.

"It must be pretty amazing," I say.

"The butterflies are like fairies," he says. "Like magic."

"We're going to do a whole unit on them in science class this year!" Autumn, another fifth grader, says. She's on the balls of her feet, bouncing.

"Are they like . . . really magic?" I ask, because I've never seen anyone so excited about butterflies before. "Are there hundreds of them? Or really big ones or something?"

The girl leans close to me. "We'd never seen butterflies before Veena's mom came up with the idea," she says. "My parents saw them when they didn't live here. But there weren't any in Eventown. So for us they're sort of like magic."

I'd been so in awe of everything Eventown *does* have, it hadn't occurred to me that maybe there were some things Eventown doesn't have. Would I have noticed the lack of butterflies, though? I'm not sure. I love them when I see them, but otherwise I don't think about them at all.

I'm about to ask Naomi if she'd ever noticed a lack of butterflies, but before I get a chance, Dad sees us. He's talking to a group of gardeners and people in fancy suits, but as soon as he notices Mom, Naomi, and me, he waves.

"My girls!" he says when he's made his way over to us. "What are you all doing here?"

"We brought breakfast," I say. "It was too good not to share."

"And we wanted to see what you're working on," Mom says.

"I'm talking them into peach roses," Dad says. "Peach roses and long grasses with a gazebo in the middle, covered in vines. Maybe a pond. Lily pads. All that."

"Frogs?" I ask, thinking of Veena's backyard and the frog she'd promised us.

"You never know," Dad says, but I don't think he's envisioning frogs for the garden. Maybe frogs are best in backyards. I don't know as much about making things beautiful as Dad does, after all. "Now. Let's see this breakfast you brought."

I hand him the cold pancake. I want it to be as delicious for him as it was for us this morning. He takes a big bite, and when he does he shuts his eyes tight like he's trying to see the taste as clearly as he feels it. I love watching Dad eat my food. Even when it's weird or wrong or too out there, Dad closes his eyes and thinks about it for a long time.

"Now that's a pancake," he says. "This is maybe the greatest pancake of all time. Hall of Famer. And I've got just the thing for your next creation." He heads back over to the group of gardeners and speaks to one, who goes to one of the patches I'd noticed earlier. He picks something from a vine.

Dad carries it back to me with a sneaky grin on his face. When he shows it to me, it's a green strawberry.

"It's not ripe," I say.

90

"It is. It's just green," Dad says. "Another Eventown specialty. Even better than blueberries. Have a taste."

I take it and bite in. It's delicious. Tangier and airier, somehow, than a red strawberry. "What do you think?" Dad asks.

"I can taste the green," I say.

"Yes! Me too!"

"I think it would be good with basil. And maybe whipped cream? Or maybe I can even make some sort of sauce with it, for fish? Or green strawberry bread. Or soup! Green strawberry soup!"

"You're a genius," Dad says. He looks so happy out here in the sun, surrounded by growing things and us.

"I bet there's some green strawberry recipes in the box, too," Mom says. I don't respond. I don't care what's in the box; the point is for me to figure out what to do with this shocking new taste.

"I can't believe this is just growing right here in town."

"Better than a boring old supermarket, right?" Dad says.

"So much better," I say. I don't even want to think about the Juniper supermarket with its freezing-cold aisles and screaming kids and cranky shoppers and fuzzy announcements about deals on frozen meals over the intercom system.

We don't need to remember any of that, I think. "Let's never think about that market again," I say.

Dad tilts his head and opens his mouth to say something but doesn't.

"Let's forget about supermarkets and cars and microwavable meals and the people in Juniper who gave us those stupid sad looks all the time," I say. The things I want to forget spill out without even trying. I didn't know how mad I still was at those memories until I compared them all to this moment right here, with green strawberries and fresh air and everyone treating us like we are fun to be around.

"You can forget it if you want," he says, suddenly very serious. "But you tell me if you ever change your mind about what you want to remember from home, okay? You can always tell me. Even if it's something I don't remember."

After all the happiness, he's looking a little sad. A little like he misses some things about Juniper. Maybe even some of the awful parts of Juniper.

"It will still be there," he whispers, words meant only for me.

But I don't know what the words mean.

"And we'll be right here," I say, not knowing what else to say. Dad looks at the grass that will someday be his garden and the dozens of happy families strolling through town, doing nothing in particular. He looks at cartwheeling Naomi and laughing Mom, her hair shining in the sun, and he looks at me, green strawberry juice probably stuck to my lips.

"Right here. In our new home," he says in a voice that could be a hundred different things.

"Our new home," I repeat, and I think the way I say it, it sounds like a wish.

Except for the first time, it really feels like it might be more than a wish. It might be our real life.

13

Glass Rooms

The butterflies, as promised, are spectacular.

Veena and her mom show us around like it's their home, and I guess it almost is. "I've been working on this for years," Ms. Butra says. She doesn't have her straw hat on today, but she has a butterfly-covered dress, and I notice Veena's collection of necklaces has a butterfly charm one too. "I wasn't sure it would happen. It takes a while to get new things here. But the town's fallen in love. I knew they would. I always loved—" She shakes her head. "Butterflies are special. Eventown deserves them."

The butterflies are free to fly around the entire space, which is really a glass castle with glass rooms. I love that we can see the sky through the ceiling, and I love the way the butterflies sometimes land on our shoulders.

Even when they're attached to me, I can't feel them, but I still know they're there. Like ghosts.

"Can we bring one home?" I ask when a blue one lands on my arm. I like the blue ones best. They're brighter than most things in nature, and plentiful in the butterfly house.

"We have to keep them contained," Ms. Butra says. It's the same word Mom used earlier, and I still don't really know what it means. "They only want them here, at the house, not out in the town." I want to run around with the butterflies, flapping my arms like they're wings. I want to *be* a butterfly for a minute, flying around a glass castle, landing on a stranger's shoulders. But Naomi only wants to watch them. And would probably never dream of asking to bring one home.

"Why?" I ask.

Ms. Butra gives me a gentle look. "I bet you're a girl who asks why a lot," she says. She bends her knees to look me in the eye. "I was always that way too."

"Is it bad?" I ask. Something about Ms. Butra makes me feel comfortable, like I could ask anything and not upset her. She's like Veena in that way—warm and easy to be around. A Ms. Butra cake would be light and fluffy on the outside, but inside would be warm, gooey cinnamon-sugar filling.

"Some people won't like it," she says. "But I think we don't have enough of it here."

I don't know if she means in the butterfly house or in all of Eventown or maybe in the whole world. But I decide to hang on to it and be curious even if people look at me funny, like Betsy and Naomi and Mom do sometimes.

There's a special room in the butterfly house that's only monarch butterflies. They're orange and black, and when they're all together they look like flashing lights filling up a room.

Naomi doesn't say a word, but she walks around the room very slowly, taking it all in. Veena stays next to me. "They remind me of you," she says after a while.

"Butterflies?"

Veena nods. "Something new and extra-fun in Eventown." I don't think I've ever had a friend say something so nice. Jenny would compliment my outfits, and Bess always liked my cookie recipes, but I never thought any of them looked at me like I was something special. The special thing about me was always just that I'm a twin. That I'm like someone else. And isn't that sort of the opposite of being special?

"Why do you think it was so hard for your mom to make this place happen?" I ask Veena. "It seems like

96

everyone loves it. Why wouldn't they want this?"

Veena shrugs. "When you came here, you left a lot of stuff behind, right?"

I think about the room we didn't pack up and the pictures on the walls and the sled in the closet. I've been trying not to think about them, but there they are now, and I can't help missing them. I didn't want to miss them. I'm tired of missing. "Yeah," I say.

"Butterflies are something people had left behind when they came here. So bringing them in—they had to make sure it wouldn't upset anyone."

"I don't understand." We're speaking quietly, but still the butterflies are avoiding us, like they know we're talking about something important and they don't want to inter-rupt. Veena sighs, and I think I'm annoying her for the first time since we've arrived. I look at Naomi, sitting and smil-ing at butterflies. I wish I could be more like her sometimes. Or even that she could be more like me.

"It's okay to not understand," Veena says, and from the way she says it I can tell she's heard something similar many times in her life. "Right?" she asks.

I nod, but I'm not sure I agree.

When I was learning to cook I was told to ask as many questions as I needed to so I could understand how to do everything. I was told that was the best way to figure it all out.

I thought everything was like that, maybe, but I guess not.

The butterflies don't ask any questions about why they're in a glass castle, staring out at dozens of rosebushes and pine trees and hills in the not-too-faraway distance. They don't ask why they're all of a sudden here and not back in their old homes, and I guess I shouldn't ask that either.

Because we're all—me, Naomi, my parents, and the butterflies—pretty happy in this new home. We have everything we need here, so why make a big fuss?

"Wanna be a butterfly with me?" I ask Veena. She grins. She may not ask as many questions as me, but she's not as shy as Naomi. She nods. We both get up and flap our arms, and for a minute they really feel like wings, they really feel like they could lift us way up in the air. We make the same lazy paths around the house as the butterflies do. Naomi watches, blushing, mouthing at me to stop. But I'm not going to stop anytime soon.

Veena laughs and follows me.

And it feels good, to run and laugh, but something is missing. A piece of me. I'm trying to be as brave and free and careless and questionless as the butterflies, but my brain won't stop asking questions, and my heart won't stop its missing.

I'm half here and half somewhere else. Not really like a butterfly at all.

14

The Opposite of Worry

That night, I make a perfect lasagna and a perfect green strawberry salad using recipes from the box. Mom, Dad, and Naomi tell me a hundred times how much they love it.

"It's not really me," I say, because the part of cooking that is me is the part where I make stuff up or improvise. Anyone could follow a bunch of recipe steps. Mom and Dad and Naomi don't understand, though. They tell me I'm being humble and ask for seconds.

After dinner Naomi and I go out to the front lawn. I like to watch stars and Naomi likes to do her routines under the cover of night. Back in Juniper, after dinner, Naomi would make up her own routines—gravity-defying ideas that worked on the lawn but she was sure would never actually work on the beam. If we caught Mom and Dad peeking out the window, we'd stop and pretend to be doing something else—naming constellations, waving at a passing car, playing tag.

"We should just lie out and watch stars," Naomi says tonight. "You like that."

"I like watching you practice," I say.

Naomi shrugs. "I don't need to practice tonight," she says, and lies down on the grass. I lie down next to her. Above us are more stars than there ever were in Juniper. They're brighter too.

"What is going on up there?" I say, staring at the sky. "You see those things? They almost hurt my eyes."

"They're huge," Naomi says.

"It's like they're miles closer," I say. "In Juniper they looked all dim. They're bright here. Like Christmas tree lights."

"It's like they're all the North Star," Naomi says. We learned a few years ago about the North Star, the brightest one, and it's my favorite.

"If I were a star, I'd want to be the North Star," I say.

Naomi laughs and shakes her head. "Of course you would," she says.

I squint, trying to find the extra-bright light, the magical bit of something special in the sky. It's not there. Or, I guess, it is there, but it blends in with all the other stars' bright lights.

"I like the way the sky looks here," Naomi says. "It's like the night isn't quite as dark."

We're both quiet for a while after that. Listening to crickets and the beating of our hearts.

"Why'd you say you don't need to practice?" I ask after a long while.

"Oh," Naomi says. "I'm sort of perfect now." She laughs, but she doesn't take it back or tell me she's kidding.

"What does that mean?" I ask.

"Just what I said," Naomi says. "I don't have to practice. I'm already doing everything right. The coach said I don't need to change anything."

I laugh. "I don't get it."

She shrugs.

"There's no such thing as perfect!"

"How would you describe your lasagna today?" Naomi says. She rolls onto her side so that she can look directly at me. "What would you call the roast chicken you made? The French toast?"

"Good," I say. "Really good."

"Come on."

"Better than anything else I've made," I say. I think

101

about the way the cheese melted on the lasagna. How there were no burnt parts. I love cooking, but usually when I'm trying new recipes, there are burnt parts.

"Elodee."

I think about the way the chicken's skin was crispy but the inside was moist. The delicate ratio of cinnamon to sugar on the French toast. The fact that every meal looked like it jumped out of a magazine and onto our plates.

In Juniper, I wasn't good at presentation. I put things on the plate all sloppy, and when Naomi would wrinkle her nose at the mess I'd say, *Taste it before you make that face.*

But in Eventown, Naomi doesn't have to wrinkle her nose.

"It's the recipe box," I say. "It helps me make everything . . . well . . . okay, fine. Perfect."

"There you go," Naomi says. She stretches her legs up to the sky and points her toes. "That's why I don't need to practice. What's there to practice?"

"Let me see," I say.

"I just want to lie here for a while," she says. "I want to look at the moon."

The moon is brighter here too. It has a special shine on it that I never noticed in Juniper. And maybe that's all it is—maybe I just notice more here. But it makes everything outside of Eventown feel even farther away. The moon is

102

supposed to be the same everywhere, everyone on the planet seeing the same glowing shape in the sky.

A little bit of worry sneaks into me. With a different moon, and a hidden North Star, it feels a little like we're lost here. And I don't exactly miss anyone in Juniper, but I don't like the feeling that things are *so* different here, that *we* could be so different here.

I want to be under the same sky we've always been under. I want some things to change, but other things to stay exactly the same.

"Do you ever worry—" I start, but when I look at Naomi, she cringes at the word *worry*. She's never liked to think much about big things or sad things or things that we have to unwind and untangle to totally understand. She's not that kind of sister, no matter how much I sometimes wish she could be. I decide to stop myself. "Never mind."

"I'm so tired of worrying, Elodee," she says. "Can we un-worry now? Can we opposite-of-worry?"

"What's the opposite of worry?" I ask, because I want to try to give Naomi what she wants. Twins are supposed to do that for each other. Especially now.

Naomi thinks for a great long while. I get lost in star patterns and the smell of Dad's rosebush next to us. I start to wonder if Naomi's fallen asleep. She's been known to do that when we're watching the sky. It makes her relaxed and sleepy, while it makes me so curious it wakes me right up.

She's not asleep, though. Her voice breaks through the light of the moon and the sweet smells.

"Hope," she says. "The opposite of worry is hope."

I nod.

And try to hope.

15

Sticky Marshmallow Sadness

Sunday night is the monthly town bonfire.

Veena and Betsy made sure we were coming when we met them in the park for cheese sandwiches and a game of kickball with some other kids from class this afternoon.

"The bonfire is my favorite night of every month," Ms. Butra says when she pours us big glasses of lemonade after the game. "Everyone all together. The world's even prettier when you see it by firelight, don't you think?"

I'd never thought about it, but she might be right.

I hope she's right.

"Dad?" I ask now as we help Dad water the rosebush. "Do you think the world is better when it's lit by firelight?"

"Better?" Dad asks, tilting his head. "I don't know about that. But it's nice to see things in a new way."

I have more questions to ask, but Dad's too distracted by his roses to explain what he means.

"Look at this thing go!" he says. The bush from back home is hard to tell apart from the other bushes now. The blooms are as red as the other bushes, as full and as pretty.

"It fits right in," Naomi says, and I can see from the glint in her eyes and the tilt of her head that she wants to be like that rosebush. She wants no one to be able to know that she came from somewhere else and used to have a whole other life.

"I can't get over the soil here," Dad says. "Magic. Now that I know how fertile everything is, I'm thinking a little fruit-tree orchard by the library. Apple trees. Pear trees. A bunch of lemon trees. Think the town will go for it, Grace?"

Mom's over in Victor and Maggie's yard, laughing at something Maggie is saying. I keep waiting for Baxter to come out so I can show him the roses or ask if he's going to the bonfire too. I like the way he seems smart and safe and goofy.

Exactly the kind of person I like most.

Mom finally looks our way.

"Go for what?" she calls back to Dad.

"My fruit trees!"

"I'm sure they will," Mom says, shaking her head a little at how much Dad loves talking about plants.

Thinking about the fruit trees gives me a great idea for the bonfire. "Bananas!" I say. "We can bring bananas to put inside the s'mores. And cookies instead of graham crackers. And peanut butter instead of chocolate!"

Once I start, I can think of a dozen different ways to make s'mores. Caramel s'mores and fruit s'mores and ice cream s'mores and pancake s'mores.

"Maybe we can do all the experimental stuff next time?" Naomi says. "Maybe we can just show up and do whatever they're doing this time?"

I roll my eyes at my sister. "People will love it," I say.

She rolls her eyes right back.

I pack one of Mom's tote bags full of ingredients I find in the kitchen that I'm convinced I can incorporate into s'mores. I've baked a batch of gingerbread, too, because there was a recipe in the box and I'd never tried to make it before. And there was something sort of fun about making a December dessert in the middle of March.

Mom brings a blanket to sit on, and Dad brings a thermos filled with hot chocolate, and we are ready for a perfect night.

We can hear the bonfire before we see it. The whole

town's there, from what it sounds like. There's a lot of laughter and someone playing "The Eventown Anthem" on a guitar and the crackling sound of fire, and then it comes into view: orange flames and everyone in comfy sweaters dangling sticks with marshmallows over the fire. It smells like the best kind of summer night—firewood and burning sugar and pine trees.

I beam at my parents. "I'm glad we're here," I say, because I know we complained about moving all the time before we came, and I want them to know they were right. This was right.

Betsy and Veena run up to us, spotting us before we reach the fire. Veena's got sticks and marshmallows all prepared for us, and Betsy right away starts telling us how to guarantee a perfectly toasted marshmallow. I try to catch Naomi's gaze to roll my eyes, but Naomi is rapt. I remember with a kind of sticky, marshmallow sadness that she doesn't like hers burnt the way I do. She's not the person who showed me how to pick up the flame and blow it out right when the sugary skin turned black.

"You're here!" Veena says, and pulls me into a hug.

"Of course we are," Naomi says. "It's tradition, right?"

Betsy beams like Naomi has gotten the answer right on some test, and I know Naomi's proud to feel like she's up on all the Eventown traditions, but I don't mind that it's unfamiliar to me.

Veena introduces me to a few of the families closest to us. They all say they've met my mom and they're happy we're here. There are cozy blankets on every bit of ground near the fire and everyone's pouring steaming chocolate into mugs and smiling and pointing out constellations to each other, just like Naomi and I always do.

It feels so homey I almost forget about my s'mores ideas. We eat three rounds of regular ones before I think to bring out my peanut butter. Veena's the first one to notice, and she leans in to see what I'm doing as I spread the peanut butter onto a graham cracker and nestle my toasted marshmallow into the center. But soon other people close by get interested, too, and watch me take the first bite. It's extra-sticky from the combination of peanut butter and marshmallow, but I like how the smokiness of the marshmallow pushes against the nutty sweetness. The taste gives me a little jolt of excitement. It tastes like *fun*.

"Delicious!" I exclaim, assuming they're all waiting on a verdict. "Who wants to try?"

I hold out the jar of peanut butter, waiting for everyone else to lean over and grab some for themselves.

They don't.

Even Veena only folds her lips together and looks into the fire instead of at me.

"I promise it's really good!" I say. "I brought cookies too. I thought they might make a good base. I mean, marshmallows on cookies, right? How could that not be amazing?"

The silence persists. Across the bonfire, people are still chatting and joking and twirling their marshmallow sticks around and around to make sure they get a perfectly even tan on all sides. But by us, there's just an awkward pause in conversation. Even in movement.

Naomi scoots closer to Betsy. I shouldn't be surprised. When I do something that she considers embarrassing, Naomi doesn't stick up for me. We've fought about it a million times, but she won't change. I'm on my own if I do something that makes me look weird.

And I guess peanut butter s'mores are making me look weird.

I take another bite of my masterpiece. It really is so good, I want everyone else to get to try it too. I hold it out to Veena. Maybe the problem is that people just don't want to put it together themselves? Or feel bad using my peanut butter? But Veena shakes her head and puts a hand on my knee like I need to stop.

"Let's just do it the regular way," she says. She looks like she feels bad about it, and I don't want to make her feel worse, so I stop. I put down the peanut butter s'more that no one will try. And as soon as it's out of my hand, conversation picks up again, sticks start twirling, Naomi visibly relaxes.

"People sort of—they take tradition really seriously," Veena whispers. "We sort of don't mess with it. Even if—even if it would be fun to try something new. It's like . . . no one's getting a palm tree for Christmas, even though it could be kind of cool, you know?"

I nod. She's right, about the palm trees.

And even I like traditions.

But I don't like the itchy way I feel, being stuck making only one kind of s'more even though I can think of twenty different ways to do it.

And I don't like the looks Naomi's giving me. Like I already ruined everything in Juniper and I sure better not ruin everything here too.

Veena makes me another regular s'more. It tastes good, but it's nothing special.

I try to focus on the smell of the fire again, and the way it's almost cold but not quite—perfect bonfire weather. Dad gives me a few sips of hot chocolate, and it's warm and rich and makes a lot of things feel better, but not everything.

Definitely not everything.

Someone starts a game of kickball, and Veena tells me I have to be on her team.

"Oh, that's okay," I say. "I'm not very good. And I think maybe—I was sort of—people seem sort of mad at me."

Veena shakes her head. "Mad?" she asks. She shakes her head again, harder this time. "Everyone wants you to play. I'm positive."

I look to where the game's begun, far enough from the fire to be safe, but close enough to still be lit up by the flame. A few of the kids wave, and maybe the wave is only for Veena, but I decide it could be for me too.

Veena runs toward them. The way she runs is like her body is air. The way she runs, her hair looks like a superhero cape behind her. The way she runs makes me want to run too.

So I do. I run right after Veena, and away from the moment we were just in. I run away from the peanut butter s'mores and the funny looks and the itchiness I felt inside. And I run toward something different and better and lit up by the biggest bonfire I've ever seen in my life.

When we play, I'm just as good as everyone else.

Better than I'd thought I'd be. Good enough to fit right in.

The best part, though, is the running.

16

Pointed Toes, High Leaps

In the morning, I try to think about kickball and my fast feet moving across the ground. But really I'm still thinking about the s'mores.

"Why do you and Dad and Naomi know how to do everything right here, but I don't?" I ask Mom over a buttery lemon scone.

"Oh, honey," Mom says. "You're doing a great job. Being new is hard."

"I feel like I keep messing up."

Mom waves her hand, which is something she often does when I say things that hint at me being sad or lonely or mad. I know trying to talk about it will just make her try to talk about a hundred other things instead.

"I think it's time for you girls to go to the Welcoming Center. I'll take you after school, okay? Things will be much easier after that, I promise."

I can't imagine what might be at the Welcoming Center that would make being new in this mysterious world easier. Maybe a rule book? A class?

"We can't go today," Naomi says. "There's my gymnastics meet."

"Oh, that's right!" Mom says. "Well, then, after school tomorrow. After you become an Eventown gymnastics champion."

Naomi blushes and I give her a one-armed hug. She squeezes me back, and I think maybe she's even more relieved than I am that there's something to help me do a better job at knowing how to fit in.

In school, no one brings up my missteps from last night, so I try to let them go and focus on History of Eventown. We're learning about how Eventown came into being, and I laugh when I hear Ms. Applebet say the name of the Eventown founder. I ask her to repeat it, to make sure I heard her right.

"Jasper Plimmswood," she says, liking the way the syllables fit together almost as much as I do, I think.

"I like it," I say. Everyone laughs, but not at me. They

laugh and nod, like they're all hearing what I'm hearing in his name.

"It's a good one," Ms. Applebet says. "And he was a special man. He lived in a town that got hit by a massive hurricane. His home was destroyed. His neighbors' homes too. It was a tragedy for his little corner of the world."

"What's a hurricane?" Charlie asks.

"That's a question for science class," Ms. Applebet says with a sigh. "But it's a type of weather that can do a lot of damage to homes and even the people in them. We don't have them here."

Charlie nods, relieved.

"Anyway," Ms. Applebet continues, "Jasper Plimmswood brought his family and his neighbors to Eventown, in the hopes of a fresh start. He wanted everyone to start over, and to let go of the pain of their past, the tragedy of the hurricane. He founded Eventown on the hope that even if something terrible happens, there's always a new leaf to turn over."

"We're going to study more about Jasper Plimmswood over the next few weeks. And learn more about all the things he did to make Eventown the special place it is today."

I think I'll be happy just hearing his name over and over the next few weeks.

Plus, I'm ahead of my classmates already, because I

115

know what a hurricane is. "Naomi," I whisper when Ms. Applebet has her back turned. "Remember the hurricane in Juniper? When our tree came down?"

Naomi nods, but she doesn't offer up her own memories, the way we usually do when we're remembering the things that have happened to us together. I want her to remember something else—the way she stood in the rain, even when Mom was yelling at her to come inside, how we painted pictures of the hurricane as if it were a real person, the moment when all the lights went out and Mom screamed so loud she made the rest of us scream too. Naomi and I have told the story of the hurricane a thousand times before, and we always share the load.

This time, though, she leaves the whole entire story to me.

I don't like it as much when it's only mine and not ours.

If she won't share the story with me, it's almost like I have no one at all.

The thought gets stuck in my throat, with the embarrassment of last night and the wish of being a butterfly and a dozen other things I've tried to swallow down so that we can belong.

I hope that Mom's right, and after the Welcoming Center, I won't have to work so hard to fit in.

When we get to Naomi's meet after school, the gym is packed—I think almost all of Eventown must be in here.

"Is gymnastics this popular?" I whisper to Veena.

"As popular as anything else!" she says, and I want to ask what that means, but a bunch of kids from our class say hi, and Mom and Dad are set up across the gym, so I wave to them and decide not to ask any more questions.

Every girl on the floor is wearing a different color leotard. Naomi's is a bright blue and I'd say it looks great on her, but that might be bragging since it would look great on me too. They're doing the beam first, and all six of them line up near the apparatus. Naomi's third, right in the middle, which I think is a good place to be. She can check out her competition, and by the time she goes, everyone will be prepared to be amazed by her. And everyone who goes after her will be a letdown.

I sit on my hands to keep them from dancing around in excitement. I love watching my sister and I love watching other people watch her too.

The first girl on beam is in pink and she does a pretty routine filled with pirouettes and a double cartwheel and a back handspring and finger flourishes and high leaps. It's good. She does every move precisely. There isn't a single wobble. But her mouth is in this straight line when she does it, and there's no sweat on her brow, no eyes staring down the beam the way I've seen Naomi do.

The second girl is in yellow. I'm spacing out a little during the routine, but it looks a lot like the first one. Straight legs.

Pointed toes. High leaps. Zero fumbles. She ends with the same dismount, breaks into an identical smile, even, at the end.

"I like their routine this month!" Betsy says, leaning over.

"What do you mean?" I ask.

"Their routine. I like this one. Last month's was sort of boring. This one looks complicated. It's cool," Betsy says. She sounds the tiniest bit annoyed to be explaining something to me, and I wonder why I can't seem to stop myself from asking questions. It seems like everyone would be happier with me if I stopped. I try to remember the way it felt out on the lawn with Naomi, when I promised I would stop worrying and try to un-worry, to hope.

It's hard, though, to be exactly what everyone else wants me to be. Naomi's good at that. I never have been. And someone once told me that was a good thing.

It doesn't feel like a good thing right now, though.

It didn't feel good last night, either.

When it's Naomi's turn, I focus on the blue of her leotard and the bounce of her ponytail.

She gets onto the beam like the other girls did, pushing up into a split. It's gorgeous. There are pirouettes. Double cartwheel. A back handspring. Delicate fingers dancing in the air.

It's exactly the same as the first two routines. That's what Betsy meant, I guess. They all do the same routine.

I look for the grit that Naomi usually has. The way she looks at the beam like she will destroy it with her eyes. The way she leans back a little too much at the end of a back handspring, not because she's lost control but because she's so happy to have nailed it. I look for her special little flourishes—a tiny kick at the end of a pirouette or a sneaky extra spin.

There's nothing.

She's good. She's perfect. The girls before her were perfect too. Watching them, I forget there even is a beam. No one is anywhere close to falling off or losing their balance. No one veers from the routine. No one forgets a single step.

The audience looks happy watching, but there's no suspense. No one's leaning forward in their seat or wringing their hands with worry. Not even me. Across the gym, Mom and Dad are calm too. Smiling. Nodding along with the spins, clapping their hands at the final landing, which Naomi, of course, nails.

Her smile at the end looks smaller than her smiles usually are. More careful.

She waves at me, like she always does at the end of the routine.

But I don't wave back.

17

Welcome!

The Welcoming Center is very welcoming.

Mom drops us off outside on Tuesday afternoon, after a full day of fun Eventown classes and everyone complimenting Naomi on her routine.

They complimented the other girls too. The same compliments, because they were all exactly the same.

"Aren't you coming with us?" I ask when Mom tells us to go inside.

"I've already been," she says. "This is just for you. Enjoy yourselves and be good."

"Wait, why?" I ask. The building looks the opposite of scary, but I still expected Mom to come with us, the way she does for anything official—a doctor's appointment, signing up for school, the first day of summer camp.

"I can't go back in," she says with a little smile. "I've already been welcomed. It's a one-time thing."

"Why?" I ask again. I can't think of anywhere else that you're only allowed to go one time.

"That's what keeps it so special," Mom says, like the explanation makes all the sense in the world.

It doesn't, but maybe I'll understand it after I've been.

I grab Naomi's hand. It's a little babyish, but she holds on tight and we don't let go.

The Welcoming Center is a big wooden building, like a barn, but much larger. It's yellow with a purple door, and the light hits it exactly right so the whole thing looks kind of magical, like there's a golden halo around it. Inside there are a few rooms and a loft on the second floor that I'm dying to sneak into. There are streamers and banners everywhere that have been put out just for us. *WELCOME, NAOMI AND ELODEE!* an enormous silver banner reads. There are pink streamers, Naomi's favorite color, and green streamers for me. The room is lit up by fairy lights, making the whole place feel both festive and enchanted.

I sort of can't believe what I'm seeing. It's better than any birthday party decorations I've ever had. It's so beautiful and over the top that it almost feels impossible.

"This is all for us?" I whisper to Naomi.

She's so shocked she can't even reply.

I want to stand still forever and take it in.

"Can we make our house look like this?" Naomi says at last. Her eyes are moon-wide. She shines.

"I love it," I say.

We're not even done looking at everything—there are rose-shaped balloons bouncing around all over the place, and "The Eventown Anthem" is playing from a harpsichord in the corner. There's a large wooden table in the middle of the room that looks like it was made from a tree cut this morning. On it are two steaming mugs of hot chocolate and a cake so big I could practically live in it. I don't know what's inside, but the outside looks like vanilla frosting, and blueberries on the top spell out our names.

I know before tasting it, before even smelling it, that it will be delicious.

A black man in a thick oatmeal-colored sweater and a white woman in a red plaid dress approach us. "Welcome!" they say at the same time.

"Thank you!" Naomi and I say back, also at the same time. We all laugh at ourselves for a moment, and I like them both right away. They have that easy sort of kindness. Like they don't have to say anything or do anything; just the way they stand and look at you and smile and tilt their heads is kind and warm and generous.

"Help yourself to hot cocoa and cake and we'll all sit down and talk about what to expect this afternoon," the woman in plaid says. "I'm Christine, and this is Josiah, and we are so happy to have you join our town."

"Thank you," Naomi and I say, again in unison, and for the first time in a while, I feel that twin thing between us.

"Every year we pick one family to join our community. It's a very serious application process, and your family was this year's selection. Which means there's something really special about you."

Naomi and I exchange a glance. This is news to us. It makes sense, though, I guess. Eventown is different from other towns we've been to. Other towns look a lot like Juniper, with malls and small houses and too many cars and gas stations and concrete and people who get mad at you when you bump into them by accident or when you climb over them at the movie theater.

Eventown isn't like that. It's not like anywhere. And the people here—they're not like people anywhere else, either. They smile more and they have this ease—like they know how life's supposed to go, like they know how to be.

I never feel quite like I know how to be.

I don't say any of this to Christine and Josiah, who are looking at us like we're supposed to say something but I'm not sure what. I wish Mom had come in with us. She's good at giving us clues as to what we're supposed to do.

"Thank you. We're so grateful," Naomi says at last. Christine and Josiah light up from this, so I try to think of something similar to say.

"I'm glad you chose us and not some other people!" I say. It's not quite as elegant as what Naomi said, and I can see that it doesn't land as well, but they're still smiling and the whole place still smells like roses and cake, and the harpsichord makes me feel a little like I'm flying around the universe instead of sitting right here.

"You seem like lovely girls, and we know a lot about your parents and, well, your life from before." She gives us a meaningful look. It makes me squirm. It makes Naomi take a big inhale. "And we're hoping we can learn a little more about your life before today. Part of our welcoming you to town is making sure you're able to start fresh here in Eventown. We want to help you say goodbye to everything that made life before hard and we want to know how best to help you get used to things here. I know that can sound scary, but it's actually sort of a nice process."

I can't sit still in my chair. I keep adjusting myself, trying to find a new position, and my feet are dancing without my permission. Naomi is the opposite. She's a statue.

"It sounds strange, I know," Josiah says. He laughs a

little, and the sound makes me relax. "I moved here from another place too. And when I was welcomed, I was right around your age. I thought the people telling me about the town were nuts."

Naomi and I let out little laughs. Something in me gives in. Maybe my heart. I like Josiah, and I love that he came here when he was our age. It's less lonely, knowing there are people like me and Naomi living here still. People who love Eventown so much they stay forever.

"The founder of the town—" Josiah begins.

"Jasper Plimmswood!" Naomi interrupts like we're in the middle of a pop quiz.

"That's right," Christine says, smiling.

"Jasper Plimmswood and the first settlers here needed to start over. Their whole lives had been destroyed by a hurricane. And living amid all that destruction, being in the place where they used to have everything and now had nothing—it was too much. They wanted to be able to be somewhere they didn't feel that loss all day every day. Somewhere they could feel whole again. And a little new. Like a big breath of air after you've been underwater for a long time. Do you know what that feels like?"

"Naomi and I have holding-our-breath contests sometimes," I say. "And when we finally give up and take a breath again, it feels great."

Christine nods eagerly.

"That's a little what Eventown feels like, I think," Josiah says.

I think about the way the stars look so bright and how somehow the sunset and sunrise seem to last forever. I think about how music class is actually fun, and I make delicious meals whenever I'm in the kitchen, and when I wake up in the mornings the day usually feels light instead of heavy, even if something hard has happened. I think about our rosebush, and how it's brighter and happier here than it ever was back home.

I think I'd like to be a little like that rosebush. Fitting right in with Eventown. Getting more beautiful and stronger and healthier in the sunlight.

"That sounds nice," Naomi says.

I nod. It does. It sounds nice. Maybe I wouldn't be so angry if I took a fresh breath. Or so lonely. Or so sad when I think about the things we don't have anymore.

"Wonderful," Christine says. "Let's get started then, shall we? I heard you two loved stories in your old town. Books with stories in them. Is that right?"

We nod.

"Then this will be easy," Josiah says, picking up right where Christine leaves off. "We're going to take you into what we call a Storytelling Room and have you tell us six stories from your life. Big stories. The story of your most scared moment, your most embarrassed moment, your most heartbreaking moment, your loneliest moment, your angriest moment, and your most joyful moment. I know that sounds like a lot. But we'll help you. Okay?"

We nod again, slower this time, foreheads a little more wrinkled.

"Oh, you girls look so scared," Christine says in the softest, gentlest voice. A cloud voice. A blanket voice. "I know everything's so new right now. But I promise there's nothing to worry about." She has deep dimples that never really disappear. "We've done this a hundred times. And it's always a good thing. Okay?"

"I'm not scared," Naomi says, even though I know she is. She just wants to do the right thing, the thing they're asking of her.

"Well then, why don't you come with me and Josiah first, okay? And Elodee can head in after. Did I get it right? You two really do look alike. It's just lovely."

"You got it right," I say, thinking it's weird how we can look so much alike when it seems like we're getting more different every day.

Naomi gets up with the straightest back and the deepest breath and looks to me. Her pretend bravery fades, and she's my regular sister again for a minute: quiet and small and nervous and needing me. I get up and give her the biggest, strongest hug I've mustered in months.

Naomi is gone for a long while. Hours, I think, but it's hard to say because I am busy eating cake and drinking hot chocolate and using the watercolors Josiah brings out for me to paint my favorite parts of Eventown. I paint the butterfly house and Veena's mother's lemonade and the ice cream shop. I paint our backyard and Naomi's smile.

I try not to think about the six stories I'm going to have to tell. How do you know which story is the scariest or loneliest? The only story I'm sure about is the most heartbreaking one.

When Naomi finally comes back to the main room, she looks rosy-cheeked and calm, just like the picture I've painted of her. She looks tired, too, but not in a bad way. She looks the way she looks after a long day at the beach or when she's won a really tough gymnastics competition.

"Elodee, you're up!" Christine calls.

"Is it weird?" I ask Naomi.

"Yeah," she says. "It's weird. But also sort of nice. To think about all the stories we have, and then to just sort of . . . let them go."

"Let them go?" I ask. There are some things I can't imagine letting go of. Deep down stories. Stories that live in my heart and in my limbs and even in my toes and fingertips.

Naomi looks out the windows, to the Eventown Hills, and maybe somewhere beyond too. "I can't explain it," she says. "But it's good. I promise. And everyone in town's done it."

I promised someone long ago that I would never simply do what everyone else was doing.

Josiah and Christine are waiting for me by the door to the room Naomi just exited, and Naomi is standing so close to me she almost feels like part of me in a way she hasn't in years, and I have a thousand stories swimming around my head all the time, and a few that tell themselves to me over and over and over no matter how hard I try to make them stop.

"I'll try," I say, so quiet only Naomi can hear me. So quiet I hope no one else hears me, especially the person I made my long-ago promise to.

18
The Perfect After

The room is the coziest I have ever been inside. Centered around a crackling stone fireplace and filled with vases of roses and bowls of blueberries, it feels both like home and like somewhere entirely made-up.

The only thing on the walls is an enormous wood carving of a rose. It's mesmerizing—the petals create a sort of spiral shape, and the wood looks both heavy and delicate. Christine must see me staring at it, because she puts a hand on my shoulder and looks at it with me.

"Beautiful, isn't it?" she says.

"Yes," I say, but it's so much more than beautiful. It's magnificent.

"Sit wherever feels comfortable," Christine says. There's a low, blue couch and a wooden rocking chair that looks like it was made by someone's grandfather. There's a small swinging hammock and a pile of cushions and an overstuffed armchair that looks like it could swallow me up.

I want to be swallowed up by rose-colored velvet cushions and thick navy blankets, so I sink into that armchair. It's heaven. A little sigh escapes as I nestle into it, lifting my knees to my chin and wrapping my arms around my shins so that I'm a tiny, cozy ball of limbs.

"I chose the chair when I came for the first time too," Josiah says, like it's a secret thing we share.

"What'd Naomi choose?" I ask. I want him to say she chose the chair, too, and sat in it just the way I am now.

"The couch," Josiah says. Christine gives him a look like maybe he wasn't supposed to tell me that. My heart sinks. The couch looks stiff and uncomfortable. The back is low and the seat is narrow. It would be hard to curl up onto it. She would have had to sit straight up on the couch, and it's hard to explain why I feel sad that Naomi would want to be perfect instead of comfortable, but it makes my eyes fill and my heart pound.

Josiah catches sight of my face, and he kneels down next to the armchair.

"Hey," he says. "It's okay. Things are going to get so

much easier for you. For both of you. That's what we all want here. To make things easier. Simpler. More even. Okay?"

The tears are falling without my permission. I nod.

"Good," Christine says. "Now, take as long as you need with each of the six stories. We want to know every detail you can remember. Every feeling and every word and every moment. This is all about you and how special the moments of your life are."

I nod again. After months and months and months of being in a family that doesn't want to talk about anything, months of not being allowed to bring up certain memories, certain details, certain bits of the past, I am excited to remember out loud instead of only, always in my head.

"You're a brave girl," Josiah says.

"I've been told that before," I say, thinking of a day at the top of a rock, looking down on a lake, being told to jump into the water, hesitating, then letting myself go. I am thinking of how much I loved the splash of water, the sinking down and bobbing back up, the grin at the end of it all, the way it felt to do the thing I'd been so scared of, the not having to be scared anymore.

"Well, maybe you'll tell us about who told you that," Josiah says. He winks again, and he doesn't look anything like my dad, but he reminds me of him anyway.

"You ready for the first story?" Christine asks. She leans forward and touches my knee. I nod. I am doing a lot of nodding in this pretty little room. "Wonderful. Why don't you start by telling us the story of the time you were most scared?"

"Take your time," Josiah says. "It might take you a minute to come up with the right story. There's no rush."

I close my eyes. The armchair gives a little more, and I could almost fall asleep, but I won't because I'm thinking through every time I ever got scared. I have no idea how I'll choose. But just when I'm trying to decide between my first time going the hospital because I burned my finger while cooking and the day I tried out for the school play, I realize there's a deeper down fear that isn't the same as being scared of doctors or singing in front of all my friends.

"I got it," I say. "It was less than a year ago. September. And we had missed the first day of school. So we were going in a week late. And I guess I sort of knew everyone would be looking at me. I mean, people look at me a lot anyway because I'm always doing things no one else is doing. Like, I like wearing skirts and dresses over jeans, and people thought that was really weird, but I just liked the way it looked. And I made friends with kids in younger grades; people thought that was weird too. Sometimes I wore stickers on my cheeks and sometimes I brought really strange things in for lunch.

Delicious things that I made with—with my family. Things they thought made no sense. Ham sandwiches with cream cheese and pickles. A container of strawberry jam to dip my apples in. I don't know, stuff like that. So I was used to people looking at me for those kinds of things. But usually they liked it, I think. They'd try the sandwich and realize it was good. Flora even started wearing skirts over pants too. My weird things weren't actually that weird.

"But this day was different. I didn't want anyone looking at me. I didn't want them asking how I was doing or if I was okay or where we'd been the week before or what I did over summer vacation. I didn't want to answer anyone's questions. And I would have been scared anyway, but then Naomi got sick. I couldn't tell if she was sick-sick or just scared-sick, but she wouldn't get out of bed. I was all dressed in my jeans and this green dress over it and a yellow cardigan over that, and I had packed my favorite lunch of a cheese-apple-bacon sandwich, and I had worked on my Everything's Fine face for hours the night before in the mirror.

"But Naomi was in bed, and refusing to move.

"Mom told Naomi she had to go to school. I could tell Dad wasn't so sure about it, though. He kept pacing back and forth across the hallway. He asked me three times in a row if I'd be okay at school by myself. I wanted to say yes, I could do anything, absolutely anything at all. But I couldn't get the words out. I was stuck to the ground. And my heart was stuck to the back of my throat. And my hands were stuck together in front of me, twisting around each other.

"The back of my neck started to sweat. Then the back of my knees. Why does it always start on the back of every-thing? Fear comes from behind I guess? It's so sneaky.

"Finally I went into our room and just begged Naomi to come with me. I was shaking and crying, and it was awful because she was crying, too, and she really wanted to stay in bed, and she really needed me to be brave and go to school by myself and check it out for her before she went, but I just couldn't. I couldn't do it. I couldn't be as brave as I was sup-posed to be. As brave as I'd promised I would be."

I drop my head. I still wish I could have been brave enough to help Naomi. I wish I could have been brave enough to go to school alone and answer everyone's questions so that Naomi wouldn't have to.

"It's okay," Josiah says, his voice startling me out of my memory. "It's okay; these stories can be hard to tell. Don't worry. You won't have to tell it again. Not ever. The story's safe with us now."

They ask a few more questions about the story and I tell them what I can remember—the color of our bedroom, what pajamas Naomi was wearing, what I ate for breakfast, who I was most scared to see at school. I tell them about the way the sun was already bright, not like here in Eventown where it's soft for hours every morning, and how Dad looked ragged and Mom was trying to be Very Responsible and Parental. I tell them some of the questions Naomi didn't want to answer and what kinds of faces I didn't want to see. I tell them as much as I can about that day, without telling them about every other day that led us there. I tell them everything I can think of until my brain feels squeezed dry and the story is totally gone.

I feel it sort of lift out of my heart.

I feel almost lighter, as if the story weighed a lot and I've been carrying it around with me. I feel *good*. A new kind of good. Maybe this is what Eventown good feels like.

"What's next?" I ask, excited to feel even lighter, even more Eventown-ish.

Christine smiles. Josiah does, too, a big, goofy grin like he's proud of me for doing such a good job telling my story.

"We'd love you to tell us the story of the time you were most embarrassed," Josiah says.

I blush just hearing the word. I'm not even thinking of a specific time. There are so many times, they all sort of bubble to the surface and heat up my face.

I tell the story of when Naomi and I were both still doing gymnastics, before I realized that being twins didn't mean we had twin talents.

"When we got to the first competition, the first one ever, I was so confident," I say, after explaining the exact colors of our leotards and the name of our coach and everyone I could remember who was watching. "I was sure I'd be wonderful. Maybe even the best one. I don't know why I felt that way. But I started this routine on the bars and I couldn't even get onto them. I mean, I literally couldn't pull myself onto the bars to even start the little baby routine. I pulled and pulled and pulled and I couldn't get the strength. The coach had to lift me up, and by then I was so embarrassed I fell right back off. It was humiliating. And Naomi laughed. She didn't mean to. She would never laugh on purpose. But it came out, and she covered her mouth and that made it so much worse. Then she got up there and blew everyone away. And it was so much more humiliating because she looks exactly like me. So it was like . . . I was the sad Before and she was the perfect After, and you could watch the one body have two totally different sets of abilities? I don't know. I sat there watching her and just wanted to hide. Forever, maybe."

The humiliation peeks back out as I speak about it, a red flush on my cheeks, my toes pointing toward each other, my head dropping, the wish to maybe somehow disappear for a few minutes until we can all forget it's ever happened.

"Embarrassment is hard to get rid of," Christine says,

"hard to forget. It always feels so present, doesn't it?"

I nod. It feels very present right now, even though I haven't done gymnastics in years.

"Keep telling us about that day, okay? We want to know everything. The whole story."

So I reach into my memory and pull up every detail I can. How we wore our hair in French braids and that I noticed that Dad cheered harder for Naomi's success than my failure. I tell them about Naomi's pointed toes and big smile and how all the girls wanted to be friends with her and not me after that. I tell them about disappearing into the bathroom for fifteen minutes just to try to get away from all the people and feelings and embarrassment.

I tell them everything I can remember, and they listen to every last bit of it.

When I'm done, I'm not blushing anymore. My toes are turned their regular way. I can look Christine and Josiah in the eye. It's gone. The story. The way it felt under my skin. The things it did to my heart.

And the memory of it too.

Gone.

19

A Golden Glow

I feel ready to tell whatever the next story is.

"Deep breath," Josiah says. "The next story is a big one."

I nod. I'm getting good at this. The stories are coming out easily, and when they're done, they drift off, like dreams I once had.

"Tell us the story of your biggest heartbreak," Christine says in a slow, careful voice.

I swear the light in the room shifts. The sun, I think, is beginning to set.

They said they'd ask for it, but I guess I hoped they wouldn't.

"Do I have to?" I ask.

"Take your time," Josiah says. But he does not say, *No problem, you don't have to tell us that!*

"Is there something we can get you to make you more comfortable?" Christine asks. "More hot chocolate? A change in the temperature? Maybe start a fire in the fireplace?"

I nod to all of it. The hot chocolate. Making the room warmer, lighting a fire. They give me a quilt; the fire hisses, then crackles, and I get a little lost in the flames and the way they climb and flutter and are somehow both wild and contained.

They wait. They wait for what feels like hours, and I want them to tell me we can move on to the next story, or that I can tell the story of my second or third biggest heartbreak, but they don't. They only wait.

"You can tell it like a story," Josiah says. "It helps, I think. To tell it like a story that happened to someone else. 'Once upon a time, a girl named Elodee lived in a place called Juniper . . .'"

And because the way he says it makes it sound less real, and because the waiting is long and the armchair is comfortable and the flames are telling me it's okay, and maybe also because no one has wanted to talk to me about this in so long, I start to talk.

I tell the story like it's a fairy tale, like it belongs to

another girl named Elodee and not exactly me.

My throat goes dry from all the talking.

My eyes are puffy.

Sometimes I wait decades in between sentences. Sometimes I start sentences that I can't finish.

I don't know how long it takes for me to tell them everything, every last thing I remember.

There is a great pause when I'm done.

"Thank you," Christine says.

And as the story settles between all of us, it starts to fade. It lifts off from me, and my heart, finally, *finally* feels a little lighter. A little less broken with every breath.

"What's the next one?" I ask. Now that I've told the worst story I know, I'm ready for the next three stories. Christine smiles like I am brave and powerful, and maybe I am.

"Tell us the story of when you were angriest," Josiah says.

"I've been angry a lot," I say.

Christine nods, like she already knows that, like it's written all over my face. "Think of when you were the *most* angry," she says. "Take your time."

I decide on the angriest of all the angry times and start to speak, but before I get more than two words out, there's a knock at the door.

Josiah and Christine exchange a look that tells me this is unusual, so I sit up straight in the armchair and un-cozy myself.

"Come in," Christina calls.

The door opens, and Naomi's on the other side of it. "Some people are here," she says, a little scared. "Veena's mom and some other people I don't know. And they say they need to talk to you."

There's another series of looks exchanged between Christine and Josiah.

"Excuse us, Elodee, Naomi," Christine says. Josiah stays with me and Naomi until Christine calls him out of the room, too, and we're all alone in the storytelling room, the fire still burning, three of my stories untold.

I wasn't sure I wanted to do all this to begin with, but now that I've told three out of the six they said they'd ask me about, I want to tell the rest. I want to feel that release of pressure, that slow fade, that letting go.

I listen at the door, trying to hear what's going on out there. I hear a few words here and there, but not enough to tell exactly what Ms. Butra and the others are doing here.

"Too young!" Ms. Butra says, beyond the door.

"They didn't choose . . . ," someone else says, followed by a dozen more words I can't make out.

"Safe . . . ," Josiah says.

"The magic of Eventown, the promise of . . . ," Christine says.

"It's time . . . ," Ms. Butra says. "Their stories . . . our stories . . . part of ourselves . . ."

I press my ear hard against the door, but Naomi pulls me away. "Don't," she says. "Just let it be."

I step away. I don't want to argue. Not in here, with the fire and the cocoa and the untold stories sitting in my chest.

When Josiah and Christine come back, they are rushing, gathering papers, putting out the fire. They don't look upset, exactly, but they are not the same as they were a few minutes ago, listening to me cry.

"We'll have to finish this another time," Josiah says, not even quite looking at us.

"We're very sorry, Elodee," Christine adds. "We'll complete your welcoming another day. Wonderful job today. You did great."

"I—I'm leaving? Before I finish telling my stories?" I ask.

"It's okay," Christine says, but she gives Josiah a look that says it might not be. "You told us such a big story, and that's what's important. Now you two head home and take some cake with you, and we'll figure this all out later." She gives a smile that is approximately half of her old smile, and she ushers me out of the room to where Ms. Butra and a few other adults are standing.

Veena's mom gives me a sad kind of smile and the smallest of waves. Naomi bites her lip.

"You girls get home safe," Josiah says. "Don't forget the cake."

And like that, we're dismissed, and back on the outside of the Welcoming Center.

"I didn't finish," I say on our walk home.

"What do you mean?" Naomi asks. The sun is still setting, and it makes her hair—and therefore probably mine—look like it's on fire. It reminds me of the flames in the storytelling room.

"I only told three stories. Not six."

"Oh." Naomi looks a little worried. "Which ones?"

"I didn't tell an angry story or a lonely one. Or . . . what was the last one?"

"Joyful," Naomi says.

"Oh, that's a fun one. What'd you say for it?" I ask.

Naomi shrugs. "I don't know, Elodee," she says. "Let's talk about something else. I'm tired."

That's when I see it. How very, very much Naomi loves it here.

She loves it more than Juniper, not just differently than Juniper. She loves even the Welcoming Center, not just the roses and ice cream like I do. She loves it more than I love it.

I try to believe she does not love it more than she loves me.

I love Naomi's smile here. The way it comes easily and stays. The way it moves into her eyes. The way it looks like mine and makes me smile too.

On the walk home, I think about the stories I would have told for an angry moment and a lonely moment and a joyful moment. I sort through the stories like my life is a book being told to me, like Christine and Josiah said. I hear about getting a new swing set in the backyard and not getting invited to Bess's birthday party and the time I was so angry that I yelled at my own reflection, at the top of my lungs, daring it to yell back.

Some stories are harder to remember. Like the book has been splashed with water at certain chapters, making the words blurry and hard to read.

And the stories I told Christine and Josiah—those stories are the hardest ones to remember. Those pages have water all over them.

And it's spreading.

I wonder if Naomi's stories are the same. I look at her, trying to tell. She sees me watching her and smiles.

"Do you feel welcomed?" she asks. "I do. I feel like we belong, finally." There's a bounce in her ponytail and a swing to her arms. The Eventown sun is setting and it gives her a golden glow.

It must do the same for me.

I hope it does.

20
A Sweet Little Storm

I wake up Wednesday after dreaming all night of a cake. And now I know I need to bake that very cake.

"You have school." Mom laughs. "You can bake a cake after." We haven't told her what happened at the Welcoming Center. I search her face to see if maybe Christine and Josiah called to tell her, but I don't see anything different about her. Maybe they forgot all about me.

I sort of hope they did.

"It's an important cake," I say. Naomi laughs. When Naomi's in a good mood she thinks all the weird things I say and do are funny. When she's in a bad mood she wants me to hide them away. Today she is all sparkly laughs and rosy cheeks and big smiles.

"Well, you can make the most important cake in the world after lunch. It can be absolutely presidential if you like. But you can't skip school to bake, as much as I'd love a slice of an Elodee cake right now." Mom kisses the top of my head, and Dad's out in the garden tending to his perfect rosebush, and I decide not to ask when, exactly, I'm going back to the Welcoming Center to finish everything up. It was so tiring, and my voice is a little hoarse from all the talking, and I don't need to go back right away.

All I really need is to make this one cake. The cake in my head. The cake that reminds me of my most joyful moment.

I think about the cake all through school. A few times Veena has to elbow me to pay attention and Betsy has to wave her hand in front of my face to remind me to listen to her talking. I want to do nothing but talk about that cake, but I think they might not understand it. It's not a chocolate cake or a vanilla cake that I want to make. It's a jasmine–olive oil cake with white chocolate–pear frosting.

A magical, strange cake that I have made before. A cake that made me happy. A cake that now makes me a little sad.

I don't want to tell anyone what flavor cake I'm thinking of making yet. I'm worried if I say it out loud, someone in Eventown will tell me not to do it. Maybe even my own sister.

But I know, more than I know anything else, that the cake has to be made, and it has to be made today.

I think about cake the whole walk home, which I do with Veena because Naomi's at gymnastics practice. It doesn't make any sense to me that Naomi's at practice if she's already perfect, but I'm happy to have the time alone with Veena. Of all the people in this town, I know Veena's the one who might not tell me my cake is too weird to make. She's the one who might not insist on a vanilla cake from the recipe box. I look at the necklaces around her neck and search for one with a cake charm. Instead, I see a locket, and it makes my heart race. So many things could be kept inside a locket. Secrets and stories. And secret stories.

She sees me seeing it, and she slips it under her shirt.

Someday, I want to ask Veena what's inside the locket. I want to ask her about all her necklaces. But not today. Not yet.

Someday, I want to ask Veena why her mom went to the Welcoming Center when I was telling my stories. I want to know why she came there when Mom said it was a one-time thing. But I'm not sure Veena knows her mother was there at all; I don't want to be the one to tell her.

I am trying to do what Naomi asked and fit in.

"Do you bake?" I ask Veena instead of asking about her mom or her necklaces. She shakes her head.

"I eat!" she says, and I laugh. Veena isn't my twin and I have only known her a short while, but I think she might get me more than almost anyone else.

"Close enough," I say. "Can you assist?"

Veena seems to consider the question very carefully. "I can," she finally concludes. I like that Veena understands the seriousness of cake. I like that Veena doesn't ask anything more about the cake, and I like that when we're at the kitchen counter a few minutes later and I finally tell her what it is we're making—jasmine–olive oil cake with white chocolate–pear frosting—she gives another serious nod. "I'm glad you're here," she says, and I don't know exactly what makes her say it, but I'm glad I'm here too.

Someone once told me that you bring your feelings into your cooking and baking, and that must mean that today's cake will taste the way friendship with Veena does—easy and soft like velvet and surprising, like fireworks exploding in the sky when it isn't even the fourth of July.

In other words, delicious.

"Can I see the recipe?" Veena asks. She bounces into the kitchen and opens the recipe box, thumbing through all the butter-stained index cards.

"Oh. Well. There isn't one," I say.

"What do you mean?"

"It's an idea in my head."

"Oh," Veena says, unsure at first, then nodding her head, then smiling. "Well, that will be new for me!"

I don't know where to start. Usually I can do lots of baking and cooking on autopilot, the steps memorized deep down in my bones. But I'm feeling all out of it today, and I can't figure out how to tackle my idea. We have all the ingredients I need—Dad brings home bags and bags of fresh finds from the market and the gardens every day. Still, my mind stalls trying to decide what to pull out of the cabinet first.

"You said it's a cake, right?" Veena asks, while I dig through cabinets and the fridge.

"Yep. Jasmine–olive oil cake with white chocolate–pear frosting." It sounds better and better the more times I say or think it. Like a poem. Like a story I haven't told anyone yet.

Veena's eyebrows rise right up to the ceiling.

"I didn't know we could do that," she says.

"Well, I'm not sure we can," I say. "I'm having trouble coming up with a plan."

Veena gives a thoughtful nod and lets me think in silence.

I go for the bowl of fruit on the counter and pick out three pears. The idea doesn't feel quite like mine. I feel the fuzzy telling of a story deep in my stomach, another watery page from the book of stories of my life before Eventown.

Cutting up the pears comes easily. I remember the

rhythm of how to cut safely and I even remember a hand over mine, showing me how to be firm without being reckless, how to be safe and fast at the same time. I try to tell the story to myself, like I did at the Welcoming Center. *Once upon a time, Elodee learned how to cook*, I think. *The counter in Juniper was white and the knives were dull and the person teaching her smelled like flour.*

It's a story I love.

I show Veena how to sift flour, and she seems to like the rhythm of her hand pressing the sifter's handle. I melt white chocolate for the white chocolate–pear frosting, and the scent is almost too sweet.

Veena loves it. "That smells amazing," she says. "Shouldn't we just leave it like that? I mean, what could be better than regular white chocolate?"

"That's boring!" I say. "We have to make it more interesting."

"How can white chocolate be boring?"

"It's just—typical. We're making something strange."

"Oh." Veena keeps sifting the flour. She doesn't really need to, but she's taking it so seriously that I don't want to bother her.

I open a box of confectioner's sugar and the powdery sweetness fluffs up, making a cloud over the box, a sweet little storm in the middle of the kitchen.

Veena laughs. "It's so messy!" she exclaims. "I didn't

know it would be all funny and messy!"

Dad comes in for a glass of water after the pears and chocolate have been mixed together on the stove and I'm just starting to experiment with the cake batter. I don't know how much jasmine is enough or how much olive oil will be too much. He watches me pour a half cup of olive oil into the bowl. It hits the batter with a sloppy sound and I know immediately that it was too much.

Veena laughs again. "Olive oil in cake!" she says. "So weird."

"It's usually really good. But I think I messed up."

"What do you mean?" she asks.

"I put in too much olive oil, I think. I'm going to have to add something else, to balance it out."

Veena still looks confused, as if I didn't answer her question at all.

"I was thinking maybe we could go out for dessert," Dad says, watching me ponder the cabinets. "Big sundaes. Or even a slice of pie at the diner."

"I'm making dessert," I say. "*We're* making dessert, I mean. Me and Veena."

Veena smiles at being included and starts stirring the white chocolate and pears with super focus.

Dad loves my cooking and baking. I've made him birthday cakes before and that he gobbled them right up. I don't know why he wouldn't want cake today.

"It just seems like a lot of work. You should be outside, having fun."

"This *is* fun," I say. "And besides, I think we need cake today. I think we need *this* cake. I dreamed about it. Here. Taste." I give him a spoonful of the frosting, and it's not perfect, but it's good. It's two different kinds of sweet. It's extra thick, and it needs more vanilla and less chocolate, but it's good.

As soon as he swallows, his eyes light up, then squint, the way they do when he's trying to think of a word for a crossword puzzle or the name of a rare flower. He takes in the mess and our smiles and the taste and pulls up a stool, deciding to stay in the kitchen with Veena and me the rest of the afternoon. He taste tests the batter and suggests a tiny bit of nutmeg for the frosting. It doesn't work, but I like experimenting with him. Veena laughs at every idea we come up with, but she tries each of them anyway. A few times she asks why I want olive oil cake when vanilla is so good, why I want pear in my frosting when plain white chocolate is so delicious, why I want to bake a cake instead of buying one from the Eventown Bakery.

"That's not the point," I say over and over.

"So the point is just trying something and seeing what happens?" Veena asks. I can almost see her brain working.

"Right. And I like to do it whether it goes well or not."

"Especially when it doesn't go well," Dad says with a silly Dad-wink.

"Especially then," I say, and we look at each other, that one glance encompassing years of kitchen memories and messy mistakes and broken plates and exploding pies and funny tastes and delicious mess-ups.

I wish Naomi were here for the moment of remembering. It's gone so fast I could almost believe it didn't happen at all. Like hard butter turning into liquid over the stove, the stories in my head, all the years in the kitchen, turn messy and soft. They aren't quite solid anymore.

When we're finally done preparing everything, it looks wrong and smells even wronger. I know the cake's not going to be good before I even put it in the oven. The flavors aren't hanging on to each other. They're not mixing right. I've added everything I can think of—buttermilk, maple extract, more eggs, different kinds of flour—but none of it quite works.

The cake falls in the oven, the middle drooping and sagging like a crater has hit it.

It tastes like olives. I spread frosting on top, but it's too hard and it comes out in clumps that tear at the soft surface of the cake.

The kitchen smells like burnt pears and olives and too much sugar.

It's a failure.

We've been in Eventown for exactly one week and I haven't had a single failure. Each recipe has been better than the one before, better than anything I'd ever made in the past. Veena keeps eating little crumbs of it, like she hopes it will start tasting good if she keeps trying it.

When Mom and Naomi arrive home, they practically recoil from the smell.

"Oh!" Mom screeches, the all-wrong flavors hitting her nose violently.

"Gross!" Naomi says. "Did something happen with the garbage?"

"Hey, now," Dad says, patting my back. "Your sister and Veena spent all afternoon baking. Don't be mean."

Naomi and Mom stand at the door to the kitchen, eyeing the mess, covering their noses. It doesn't smell as bad as all that, but in Eventown everything has been sweet and light and delicate. Rosy. So imperfection is especially shocking.

"I wanted to make something special today," I say, hoping they'll agree and understand. I see all over their faces that they don't, though, and the loneliness sets back in, an old friend that keeps stopping by unannounced.

Naomi sticks her finger into the frosting and licks it. She cringes. Veena giggles a little, like she's been doing all day. It only takes Naomi a second to laugh too. Dad shakes his head, a low laugh coming out first, then a loud one, his hand over his belly. Naomi tries to get Mom to lick some off her finger, but Mom runs away squealing, like Naomi and I used to do when we were little and being offered vegetables.

My heart can't seem to decide between being hurt by their laughter and wishing I could feel all light and easy and silly and join in with them.

I hate being stuck between the two emotions, and I hate that they don't notice me not-laughing and not-squealing and not being one of them.

I try to muster a smile, and I think it probably comes out as droopy and wrong as the cake, but it will have to do. I don't want to ruin Naomi's smile or Mom's laugh or the way Dad is wiping happy tears from his eyes. So I let my fallen smile stay on my face and try to feel the way they do.

"Stick to the recipes," Mom says with a wink after a while.

But I don't want to stick to the recipes.

21
Shy Tulips

Monday afternoon, after school, Naomi and I are laid out on a picnic blanket with bowls of blueberries and watercolors like they had at the Welcoming Center. We're painting rosebushes, and the paintings are coming out great.

"Someone needs to know," Naomi says.

"Hm?"

"About the interruption. About you not telling all your stories."

A little flicker of nerves dances around in my chest. I'm not sure what will happen if we tell someone. "Well, we could tell Veena," I say, because I know Veena will know what to do.

"I was thinking Mom and Dad," Naomi says. "Don't you think we should let them know?"

I shake my head. "If it mattered, Josiah and Christine would tell them. They're really busy anyway, with work. We should just let it be." I try to sound casual, like the whole thing is no big deal.

I liked the Welcoming Center. I liked telling my stories. But I don't want to go back. I don't feel like telling any more stories.

Before Naomi can argue, Baxter's figure casts a shadow over the painting I'm finishing up that focuses on the petals.

"I didn't know we had famous artists next door," he says. Naomi squints, looking up at him. They haven't met yet. "You must be the other twin," he says by way of introduction. I can tell she doesn't like this, but she smiles anyway.

"Maybe Elodee's the other twin," she says. Naomi is funny like this. She says things in such a quiet voice that sometimes people don't hear the bite in it that I do.

"Maybe you both are," Baxter says, and it's the perfect thing to say because Naomi stops squinting and I start adding a Baxter-shaped figure to my watercolor.

"This is Baxter," I say to Naomi. "He's the one from next door. He's in high school."

"You want to do watercolors?" Naomi asks. She scoots over on the blanket, making room for his long limbs. She lays out a pad of paper and lifts a brush to him.

"Not usually my thing," Baxter says. "But why not?"

"You're just coming over to say hi?" I ask as he gets himself settled in between us.

"I wanted to check out your rosebush," he says. "It looked a little funny." He points to the rosebush behind us, the one from Juniper. Naomi and I both turn to follow his pointer finger. I hadn't looked very closely at it today, but I guess he's right. It looks brighter than the other bushes. The leaves are shinier. The roses are bigger. The bush looks crowded, like there are more blooms than there are supposed to be.

"Oh," I say, "how'd you even notice that?"

"Never seen one like that before," he says. He's painting the sky first. I look around to all our rosebushes and all of his and crane my neck to look at the ones across the street too. Every other rosebush in his yard and our yard and the yard across the street matches. I bet if I counted how many blooms were on each one, they would all be the same. I bet if I measured their height and width they'd all come out the same.

Except ours.

Naomi blushes, turning very nearly the color of the roses. "That's so weird," she says. "Our dad's a really good gardener. So probably he just knows how to make roses even prettier than they usually are."

Baxter smiles, but he doesn't say anything in return. He paints the sky bluer. It's not very interesting to paint a sky without clouds, but there aren't any clouds here, so he just brushes streak after streak of identical blue onto the page.

"Baxter's a gardener too," I tell Naomi. She nods but doesn't take her eyes from the Juniper rosebush. "Does anyone think your gardening is weird?" I ask our new maybe-friend.

Baxter tilts his head. "What do you mean?"

I'm not exactly sure why I'm asking the question, but it feels like something kids might do. Laugh at the things someone else likes.

"I don't know, I guess a lot of boys don't like flowers," I say with a shrug, and that doesn't sound quite right either. My dad's a boy, and he loves flowers. And I think I knew other boys who liked flowers too. I'm almost sure of it, actually.

"Everyone likes flowers," Baxter says. "What's not to like?" He leans close to one of the healthy rosebushes and breathes in the scent.

"What's your favorite?" I ask. "Mine's daisies."

"Roses," Baxter says, with a happy shrug. He shrugs a lot, our maybe-friend. He doesn't have Veena's boundless energy or Betsy's certainty. He has something else that I like, though. I just wish he would talk more.

"Well, Eventown is the place for you, then," I say.

"Roses are my favorite too," Naomi says. I prickle a little. Naomi's favorite flower has always been tulips. She used to say they looked shy, like her. Roses are too intense for Naomi. They're too dramatic. I don't correct her, though. She's already out of sorts from the Juniper rosebush looking like it doesn't quite belong.

"Do you think someone's favorite flower tells you something about the person?" I ask Baxter. Naomi doesn't always like my deep, weird questions, but I feel like Baxter will. He gets up, having finished his blue-sky watercolor. There's something familiar about the way he holds his body, the way he shifts his weight from side to side with his hands in his pockets, the way he talks to us like we aren't silly little kids but like he really wants to hang out with us. I look up at him and hope that he wants to talk about weird and deep things with me, that he wants to analyze the meanings of people's favorite flowers, that he maybe wants to sing at the top of his lungs on a walk through town even though everyone will look at us, that he would tell me to keep making my weird cake even if it tastes awful, even if no one likes it, even if it never ever tastes the way it does in my head.

I imagine Baxter doing and saying all of these things, and the fantasy of it makes me feel cozy and homey.

But Baxter—this one, the one right in front of me

shifting back and forth with his hands in his pockets—shrugs again. "What would a favorite flower tell you about someone?" he asks.

I look at Naomi to see if she'll offer up the anecdote about shy tulips and I consider telling him how daisies are sort of wild and sunny and silly like me, but I don't think he'll understand.

Instead, no one says anything at all. We drop it, and I try to put a finger on what feels so wrong about this moment right here, this moment that should be a nice one.

Baxter tells us to have a good day, and Naomi promises we will, and I stay quiet, quieter than I ever am, because I am never very quiet at all. Naomi goes back to her watercolor. It's really pretty. Baxter goes back to his side of the yard and hums "The Eventown Anthem" to himself while he pulls a few tiny, almost-not-there-at-all weeds.

So I'm the only one still looking at the Juniper rosebush. I'm the only one who sees a new bud appear. It pops up, like it's coming out of nowhere, and it even starts to open. It makes my heart gasp. It's the most incredible thing I've ever seen, a perfect little surprise in the middle of a regular day. I wish I could paint the moment, but it's not the kind of thing you can capture in watercolors.

I don't tell Naomi. She wouldn't like it.

I almost never have secrets that are entirely mine, but

that little bud popping up at the bottom of the rosebush is going to be a secret that's just mine for now. It feels funny, having it wander around inside me with nowhere else to go.

I look at Baxter's painting, and I know exactly what's missing. I tear a piece of white construction paper into the shape of a messy cloud and lay it on top of Baxter's picture. A cloud in Baxter's perfect blue sky. A rosebush crowded with huge flowers. The messy confusion of how my heart feels.

I don't think any of it is quite right for Eventown.

22

The Eventown Anthem

"What do you think we'll play in music today?" I ask Veena on our way into class that Thursday.

"What do you mean?" she asks.

"What other songs do you guys know?"

Veena tilts her head and her forehead scrunches. She opens her mouth to answer, but before she can, Betsy and Naomi come up behind us, giggling about who knows what. Betsy and Naomi have been giggling together a lot. I don't mind it, I guess, but I'm used to being the main person Naomi giggles with.

"What's so funny?" I ask.

Betsy doesn't answer. She just keeps giggling.

"I'll tell you later," Naomi says. But I don't think she will. She'll forget or tell me it's not important, and I'll pretend I don't think it's important either. But I've noticed lately the way she beams bigger at Betsy than she does at me. And the way she's started wearing her hair like Betsy's, too, a center part and a shiny barrette on each side holding the front pieces back.

"Is Betsy your new twin?" I asked her this morning, when she was making sure the pink clips were even.

"Of course not!" she said. "You're my only twin. But isn't Betsy awesome?"

I *mm-hmm*ed. And I meant it.

Mostly.

Mr. Fountain directs us to our instruments, and the music on our music stands is "The Eventown Anthem" again. It's the only song we've played for the three weeks we've been here. I do love the way we all sound playing it, so I chime my triangle with gusto the first time through.

And the second time through.

The third too. The anthem sounds like a brook, like a wood nymph running through the forest, like wind chimes. It's light and quick and perfect for the triangle.

"Again!" Mr. Fountain says when we've finished the third time.

"Again!" Mr. Fountain says, and we start up again. The

165

melody is the kind that attaches to your brain and doesn't let go, so I know I'll be humming it as I make dinner, as I try to bake my special cake again, as I try to fall asleep later tonight.

Naomi is serious at her cymbals, and even the xylophones sound sophisticated and sweet.

After the fifth time, I raise my hand.

"What song are we playing after this one?" I ask. "I think Naomi and I can try to catch up with your other songs too." I look to Naomi for confirmation and she nods eagerly.

"What do you mean?" Mr. Fountain asks. He scratches his beard. His bushy eyebrows draw toward each other.

"What other songs do you guys play? Aside from 'The Eventown Anthem'?"

The room goes very, very quiet. Mr. Fountain clears his throat and wrings his hands.

"Let's talk after class, girls," he says.

"I mean, we love the anthem! But we're happy to learn anything. We both love our instruments, so we want to try them on different—"

"After class," Mr. Fountain says. It isn't mean, not like Mrs. Jones was when I asked her when my turn to play the triangle would be. But it's abrupt, like the case is closed, like there's nothing else to say.

The other kids shift ever so slightly away from us. They shuffle their papers. They whisper something. Betsy's

166

blushing. Veena's putting her fingers to her lips to tell me to be quiet.

Mr. Fountain raises his hand, and we play the anthem again. We stumble over the harder parts, and the whole thing sounds a little less cheery. But we get through it. And still my triangle sounds like magic.

The rest of the class is very still after the rocky rendition. They're all exchanging heavy glances and fidgeting in their chairs. Betsy purses her lips. Veena plays with her necklaces. I am all wrong and I don't know why I'm wrong. It feels not unlike Monday in our backyard with Baxter looking at the rosebush or the way Naomi's face made me feel when she first looked at my messy cake or my peanut butter s'mores.

I am off-center. I am doing everything wrong. And inside, I am fuming at all of it. Mad at myself for not getting things right. Mad at Naomi for not being on the same page as me. Mad even at Mr. Fountain for looking at us funny.

Naomi's not mad. She's not sad either. She doesn't even look nervous at the mess-up. She just watches Betsy, like Betsy's movement will tell her everything she needs to know.

"Why doesn't everyone head out to recess?" Mr. Fountain says. "Naomi and Elodee, you girls are making such beautiful music, but why don't we have a quick chat?"

I swallow hard.

Naomi and I stay in the room while the rest of the class clears out. I know Naomi must be unhappy that I've made us stand out once again, but I can't apologize because she won't look at me.

"Girls," Mr. Fountain starts before taking a long pause. I get the feeling he hasn't thought through how to say whatever it is he needs to say. "First of all, welcome. Eventown is happy to have you. Eventown Elementary is happy to have you. And I am very happy to have you. You did great today."

We nod and look at the floor. I know he's being nice, but I'd rather he jump right in and tell us what we did wrong.

"Are you enjoying it here?" he asks. His bushy eyebrows scrunch up.

"Yes," Naomi and I say in unison. Mr. Fountain smiles. People love when twins say things in unison, even if it's a one-syllable word.

"And you are lovely musicians," Mr. Fountain says. He waits, as if he's asked a question that we have the answer to. But Naomi and I don't know what to say.

I try smiling, so he knows how happy we are, how well we fit in. I do it for Naomi, and a little for me too.

Naomi shifts her weight and accidentally knocks over one of the cymbals. It hits the ground with an epic, echoing crash. I talk too much and Naomi's clumsy and I love these things about us, but I know Naomi always wants to hide those things away so no one can see everything that makes us different.

"Sometimes it takes a while to learn about a new place," Mr. Fountain goes on. "And that's okay. That's perfectly understandable." Again he waits. Again, we have no idea what in the world we're meant to say.

Mr. Fountain scratches his beard. I wonder, since it's so itchy, why he doesn't just shave it off.

"Did we do something wrong?" Naomi asks.

"We didn't mean to," I add.

"Questions are great; don't get me wrong. But our town is very small. And we're not always used to questions. You didn't do anything wrong. But your question surprised me. And I think it confused your classmates."

"Which question?" I'm still whispering. I don't want anyone to hear that we messed up.

"About playing other songs," Mr. Fountain says. He says the words delicately, like they are fragile things that he doesn't want to accidentally shake or drop or break.

Naomi and I look at each other. It still doesn't make sense. Was it rude? Did it seem like I didn't like the song we were playing? I get a flutter of memory—of being in trouble back in Juniper—but the flutter stills, and I can't even remember who I was in trouble with or what was said to me or what I might have done wrong.

"The thing is, there aren't other songs here," Mr. Fountain says.

"Oh. We don't play other songs in music class?" I ask. It seems a little strange—the anthem is nice, but I'd think it would get boring to play the same thing over and over. And what happens when everyone's mastered that song? Is music class over then? Do you stop taking it? Or maybe we all change instruments and learn how to play "The Eventown Anthem" on every single instrument? That would be okay, I guess.

Mr. Fountain scratches his beard. He seems tired. The conversation seems like it's taking a lot out of him. He's not the upbeat, kind, generous, music-loving guy he was at the beginning of class. "In Eventown. There aren't other songs in Eventown."

"Really?" I ask. "I bet you know this one!" I start to sing a song I love, by the Beatles: "I Will." *Who knows how long I've loved you—*

"Oh, Elodee," Mr. Fountain interrupts. "No." He clears his throat. He puts a hand on my shoulder, and it is strong and sure and calming. "In Eventown we have the anthem. Remember Jasper Plimmswood and the fresh start? 'The Eventown Anthem' is the fresh start. 'The Eventown Anthem' is enough. More than enough. It's beautiful, isn't it?"

"Of course," Naomi answers quickly, like it's a race, and I know I'm meant to say the same thing, but I'm singing the Beatles song in my head. I love that song. My parents played it at their wedding, and we've all heard it a billion times. They sang it to us as a lullaby when we were little, and we've sung it in the car and in the kitchen and sometimes just walking down the street, almost accidentally, as if our bodies are tuned to the melody automatically.

I nearly tell Mr. Fountain about the interruption at the Welcoming Center, since he seems so confused and maybe that's what's making me do all the wrong things.

The song keeps playing itself in my head, and it makes me smile. A story pops into my head about a time I came up with a dance to it and performed it for my family and everyone learned the dance and we did it all night long.

Maybe that story was my most joyful story. Or one of a lot of joyful stories.

I don't think I want to tell it to Christine and Josiah.

For now, I only want to tell it to myself.

"I like the anthem," I say. "But I thought you might like our song from home—"

"Elodee." Naomi's voice is very strong and very clear. There is a not-very-Naomi-like urgency to the way she's saying my name that tells me it really matters to her that I be quiet.

I wonder if she's forgotten the song. She didn't light up when I started singing it. She didn't join in or look nostalgic for all the stories of the nights we listened to that song with

171

our family. I wonder if her memories, like mine, are melting like butter in a pan, changing form, boiling down, some of them disappearing completely.

I don't want her to forget it. I don't want to forget it. Since the Welcoming Center, some things feel far away and splotchy, and it's okay, I guess, but uncomfortable too. That song is something I love, something that makes me happy. And forgetting feels a little like a loss.

I want to say all of that to Naomi and to Mr. Fountain and his beard. I want to say it to Veena and Betsy and anyone who will listen and explain and help me understand why some of the stories in my head are splotchy and hazy and water damaged. I want them to help me understand why the stories I told Christine and Josiah are already gone and the ones I didn't get to tell them are thumping around in my body and no one else's.

But I don't.

Mr. Fountain plays the anthem on his piano and the tune is so light and lovely and sweet and easy that I get a little lost in it and the way it makes me feel. I feel nice again.

Nice is a small feeling. A contained one.

"It's a beautiful song," I say.

"It's the *most* beautiful song," Naomi says.

And it is.

It is the most beautiful song.

23

A Book of Nothing

Mom picks us up after school. She used to do this at home sometimes, too, and it always means something fun. She comes with a grin and a plan for adventure. Once we drove to her favorite lake and had a picnic. Once she drove us to a water park even though it was a little too cold for a water park.

The cold made it even better.

I don't think it's a water park or a picnic today, though. Mom's still in her work clothes—heels and a pretty gray skirt and a prettier pink blouse. Naomi and I use our twin powers to silently agree not to tell Mom anything about music class or Mr. Fountain or the mistake I made.

I give Naomi a thank-you look.

She grimaces, like she's not sure it's the right decision.

"The construction on the library is done," Mom says, hugging us hello. "It opens back up tomorrow, but they said I could bring you girls by today. You can explore a little bit. What do you think?"

Naomi and I light up. Back home, we used to stay at the library for hours, reading whole books on the floor, leaning against the stacks. Veena said the Eventown Library is enormous. And cozy. And her favorite thing in town along with every other thing in town.

"Is the fireplace working?" I ask.

Mom nods.

"Can we stay for a long time?" Naomi asks.

"Absolutely," Mom says. Naomi and I practically skip the whole way there. We stand outside the building for a few minutes before going in. Mom tells us everything she knows about the library. When it was built and what materials were used and all the little details that make it special.

"It's really a place for the whole community to come together," she says. "It's probably the most beautiful building in the whole town. And do you see those roses carved into the stones? And the way it looks like a huge house, instead of a regular library? It's supposed to really be like someone's home."

She's right. It looks like someone could live here, and I can't think of anything better than being able to live at a library.

Inside, it's even better. The stacks of books reach all the way up to the ceiling, and they're all leather bound with gold engraving on the spines. Even my favorite books are bound this way, and I don't miss regular covers at all. These make every book look like an artifact, look special.

"Wow," Naomi and I say together. We look at each other, laugh, and then say it at the same time again, drawing the middle *ow* sound out longer. "Wooooooooowwwwwww," we say.

"Pretty special, huh?" Mom says. "We really believe it could be a destination library. Not that destination libraries really exist in tourism, but they could! It's something we've been talking about a lot at work. Reaching families who are looking for a different kind of vacation. Homey. Safe. Special."

Back home, Mom never lit up when she talked about her job. She complained about runs in her stockings and her boss's late-night emails and her officemate's tuna fish salad and her lack of vacation days. But here Mom bounces on her toes when she talks about work. She sparkles.

It's contagious. Soon Naomi and I are bouncing on our toes and sparkling too. We run up and down the long aisles of red-and-gold carpeting. We lie on our backs and stare up at the skylight. We brush our fingers along the spines of books. We gather a few up in our arms and bring them to the fireplace. We want to cozy up in front of the flame Mom has started. We want to read for the whole rest of the afternoon and evening.

Naomi likes books about animals and magic and I like books about people and food, so we go to the cooking section and the animal section and the fantasy section and choose titles that sound right. We have a mix of everything we love, and we lie on our stomachs and bend our knees so that our feet face the ceiling. We rest our chins on our elbows and open one book each.

I turn a page.

Then another.

Another.

Another.

They are blank.

I flip through the whole book. Every page is blank. It is a book of blank pages. A book of nothing.

"This is so weird," I say. "Mom, you should tell them this book is blank." Mom's too far away to hear me, though. She's busy sorting through the stacks, lining up and rearranging books and making it all look perfect.

I pick up another book.

Blank pages. Over a hundred of them.

My heart beats louder and I look at Naomi. She's staring at blank pages too. She isn't flushed or freaking out, though. She's calm about it. She looks a little baffled but not very worried.

"Naomi?" I say. "Are you seeing this?"

I open another book from our pile.

Blank.

Another and another, all blank.

"Are we supposed to write in these? Are they like journals?" It wouldn't be quite what I wanted, which was to get lost in someone else's story, but as days pass and the stories I have from my own life get blurrier and more waterlogged, writing some down for safekeeping doesn't seem like a terrible idea.

"Oh! No!" Mom says, finally hearing me. "Don't write in those!"

"But where are the stories, then?" I ask.

"Well, it's not that kind of library," Mom says gently.

"It's sort of interesting, right?" Naomi says.

". . . No?" I say. I don't understand what she's saying at all. It's not interesting to have a library full of blank books. It's not interesting to use books as decoration. It's weird. It's terrible. It's . . . wrong.

"They're so pretty," Naomi says. "And the whole place

is kind of magical. I guess it's meant more as a place to hang out and be together and not get all lost in reading, you know?"

"What are you talking about?" Heat rises up and flushes my face.

"I'm trying to see the good." Naomi shrugs. "I don't feel like getting all worked up about something."

"Well, I don't either, but there's something to get worked up about, so I don't have a choice!"

"Okay, deep breath, Elodee," Mom says. "Let's all take deep breaths."

"I'm breathing fine!" I say. But my heart won't stop thumping. Mom puts a hand on my back. It's meant to calm me down, and it works. It always works. Mom's hands are strong and they don't shake and they're always a little cool. I'm so glad that hasn't changed. "It's different. I know. And different can be overwhelming. But I think it's special too. A place you've never been before. A place unlike any other. An adventure. Right?" She smiles, and her smile softens me the teeny-tiniest bit. Then just a little smidge more.

"But where will we get real books, that we can read?" I ask in a small voice. I don't want Mom to stop being so excited, but I'm nervous I won't be able to share that excitement with her.

"We all have so many stories inside of us," Mom says.

"Every single day is a story! Especially here in Eventown. Don't you think?"

"I don't know," I say. My brain is feeling mushy from all the strange things Mom's saying and the fact that Naomi doesn't seem as worried as me. Little bites of anger nip at me, still, but they feel wrong here. They make me feel uncomfortable and tight and they don't stick to my heart. I feel lost. I don't know which feeling to settle into, or which feeling is settling into me.

"We moved here to be something new and different," Mom says. "If we wanted a regular town like Juniper, we could have stayed in Juniper. But we're on an adventure. We're somewhere a little more special. If everything was exactly what you expected it to be, it wouldn't be so special, right?" She's giving me an extra-special, extra-long look. She wants me to see only the good, the way she does here.

Naomi nods along. "It's nice, Elodee," she says. "It's not the same as . . . as the other place . . . but it's really nice here. Magical."

I know Mom wants me to be like Naomi right now, and I want to be what Mom wants me to be, so I try to nod and smile, too, but it hurts a little. It feels a little like pretending.

We sit and listen to the fire crackle. I love the sound and the smell. After a while, my heart beats its regular rhythm. The rug is cozy, my sister is nearby, Mom is happy, and still the smell of roses drifts into the room, even here, even with the fire going.

I want the niceness, the coziness and warmth to be enough. The way it is for Mom. The way it is for Naomi. I want to fit in with them and feel all the same things in all the same moments. It would be less lonely to feel the same way as the people I love most.

Stop being lonely! I tell my heart. *Feel the right way!*

It tries. It really, really tries hard.

Before we leave, though, I peek at a few more books. Just to make absolutely sure I didn't miss something. Maybe, I think, a few of them have words. Maybe, I think, there's one tiny poem or just a beautiful sentence somewhere in this enormous building.

But every book I open up is the same.

Blank.

24

Faded Freckles

I'd almost forgotten about our birthday when Dad asks us over dinner that night what we want to do for it.

"Oh!" Naomi says, and I can tell she'd forgotten too. "What do people do for birthdays here?"

"Probably exactly what they do everywhere else," I say. I don't want to think about what everyone else thinks we're supposed to do. I want to come up with something that we'll love. Twelve seems like a really important birthday. A grown-up birthday.

"We can do anything you'd like," Mom says.

"Within reason!" Dad says, laughing.

"Within reason, yes," Mom says, rolling her eyes at Dad.

"No elephant rides or skydiving, okay?"

"No trips back to Juniper," I say. I mean to say it in the same joking way Mom and Dad are saying things, but I must do it wrong, because everyone falls silent.

"Gross. Why would we go back to Juniper?" Naomi says.

"I was kidding," I say, blushing. I wait for someone to say something, anything else so that we can all forget the bad joke I made.

"How about a tea party?" Mom says. "Something a little grown-up for such a grown-up birthday?"

Naomi and I smile the same smile at the same moment. It feels good to agree so fully about something as important as your twelfth birthday.

"That sounds perfect," Naomi says.

"You and me with Veena and Betsy?" I say.

"Yes! With little tiny sandwiches. And that tea set in the cupboard!" Naomi and I are talking quickly now. We've always loved our birthday.

"We can set up outside. A picnic tea party," I say.

"Should we wear dresses?"

"Yes, and maybe hats."

"Do people wear hats at tea parties, Mom?" Naomi asks. I bet my eyes are as shiny as hers. I bet her heart is beating as excitedly as mine.

"I think they do," Mom says. "We can find some special ones for you."

"Maybe I'll pick some special flowers for the hats," Dad says.

"Veena and Betsy will love it," Naomi says. She sighs a big, happy sigh, and I do the same. "It's going to be perfect."

And for once, I'm sure that it is.

It's hard to fall asleep, thinking about our tea-party birthday. I think it's going to be our best birthday party yet—better than roller-skating or makeovers or the year we went on a scavenger hunt all over Juniper. Those were all little-kids' birthdays. This one will be different. A fancy Eventown party with the best friends we've ever had.

"Are you up?" I whisper to the top bunk. I want to ask Naomi if she has any more ideas for food or cake or if we should organize any games.

But Naomi, somehow, is breathing heavily. Probably dreaming of our party. I sit up in bed. I can't stand lying there with my mind running all over the place. Maybe I'll be able to sleep if I go take a look at the tea set and write down a few more ideas.

I sneak downstairs. The house in Eventown doesn't creak. It's easy to silently tiptoe through it. It's sort of nice, being up by myself, and before I go to the tea set I sneak a glass of milk and a chocolate chip cookie for a midnight snack that I can eat while I look at the moon.

The whole world feels right.

When I've finished the cookie and the moon starts to get boring, I head to the cabinet with the tea set. I know it's on the highest shelf because it's the most breakable, delicate thing in the house, and Mom always puts fragile things up high *just in case*.

I drag the step stool over to the cabinet, and I can't reach the whole set, but I hook my finger around one of the teacups. I pat the shelf blindly to see if there's anything else I can reach, and my fingers find a glossy slip of paper.

I almost don't bring it down. I know that aside from fragile things, Mom and Dad sometimes put other important things on top shelves. Credit cards and letters and sometimes even presents that Naomi and I aren't supposed to see until our birthday or Christmas. Still, I can't resist. Maybe it's a birthday card for us. Maybe it's a special recipe they're saving for a rainy day.

I slide the teacup off my finger and onto a low shelf, and look at the paper in my hand.

It's not regular paper, I realize. It's shiny photo paper.

A photograph.

I try to remember if we brought any photo albums with us. Back in Juniper, Mom would keep the photo albums on the coffee table so that anyone who wanted to could flip through them and see all the best memories of the last few years. But in Eventown we only have a vase of roses on the coffee table. No photo albums.

We also don't have any family photos hanging on the walls or set up on the mantel. Nothing stuck to the fridge, either. I try to push away the feeling that there's something strange about that. Maybe we haven't unpacked our photos yet. Maybe Mom's keeping them somewhere else and if I ask her about them tomorrow it will be no big deal at all.

But something tells me that this might be the only photo in our Eventown home.

Something tells me photos are like the six tales we were supposed to tell at the Welcoming Center—meant to be forgotten.

I flip the photo over.

It's a picture of a boy a few years older than me. He has long legs and light brown hair and a funny, smirky smile. He's in a garden, using his hands to dig a new place for a little, not-yet-bloomed flower.

His nose is sunburned and he has eyes like mine. It's not a picture I've seen before. But it's a picture that feels like home anyway.

I can't place who it could possibly be. The person looks both familiar and not familiar. My heart responds to his face, even though my brain has nothing to offer. I like the boy in the picture even though I can't think of who it might be.

"Oh!" I say to myself at last. "Dad!" He has Dad's shoulders and nose and love of flowers, clearly. He looks a little like me and Naomi and a little like Dad and even a little like Mom. It must be a photo of Dad when he was young.

I've always liked seeing pictures of my parents when they were my age. So it makes sense that I would like this photograph and half recognize the person in it.

I look at it again and smile at the way younger-Dad's smile is toothier than his smile now, and his arms and legs are skinnier. I could put the photograph back in its rightful place, on the highest shelf, but I like it too much to let it go.

I'm missing the old photographs of Mom as a chubby baby and Dad going to prom that we used to look at all the time, back in Juniper. And I'm worried those photos are gone. So I have to hold on to this one, just in case.

I bring it upstairs with me. I can't stop looking at the faded freckles, the red nose, the hands digging in dirt. I don't want to stop looking at it. So I fall asleep with the photograph in my hands.

When I wake up in the morning, it's fallen right against my heart.

25
My Stupid Heart

I feel twelve when I wake up two days later, on Saturday morning.

"Do you feel twelve?" I ask Naomi when she's climbed down from her bunk.

She stretches. She wiggles her fingers. She coughs.

Finally, she smiles.

"Yep!" she says. She barrels downstairs. I wait an extra few seconds before following her. Long enough to open up the drawer of my bedside table and take a look at the photograph I found the other day. It's become a ritual the last few days. I like to look at it in the morning and at night.

I'll ask my dad about it soon.

But not yet. Right now, I like it being mine.

Mom's brought us chocolate croissants and hot chocolate and chocolate doughnuts for breakfast, and I bet the whole town can hear Naomi and me squeal with excitement at our all-chocolate breakfast.

"I thought it might be a nice new tradition," Mom says with a grin.

"I didn't know you could start new traditions," I say.

"Sure you can," Mom says. "How do you think they become old traditions?"

"This is a perfect new tradition," Naomi says. "Let's keep it."

I nod and take a big bite of doughnut. "Yep," I say with a full mouth, because on your birthday no one's going to stop you from talking with your mouth full. "Let's keep it."

Dad sings a rousing rendition of "Happy Birthday" at the top of his lungs and uses all different voices—a monster voice and an old lady voice and a little baby voice. Mom sings it regular, and that's nice too.

"Happy birthday, Omi," I say to my sister, using the special nickname like I do every year.

She looks at me a little funny.

"Happy birthday, Elodee," she replies, instead of calling me Elo, the way she's supposed to.

"We've got a lot of getting ready to do!" Mom says. She

brings out two new dresses for us and they look perfect for a tea party. Naomi's is pink and flouncy, and mine is light green with lace at the bottom. Dad brings out our flowery hats—he's made four. I choose a yellow one and Naomi chooses a pink one, and we leave a blue one and a purple one for Veena and Betsy. They have roses in the front and ribbons in the back and they're a little ridiculous but also really beautiful.

I make a huge array of sandwiches—BLTs with extra-crispy bacon, and chicken salad with apples and celery, and peanut butter and jelly with homemade blueberry jelly from our never-ending supply of blueberries.

I resist combining the sandwiches, even though I'd like to put bacon on the peanut butter or apples in with the BLT. I keep them all normal.

Naomi picks some roses and puts them in a vase in the middle of our picnic blanket, with the beautiful tea set. We don't like tea, so we fill the teapot with fresh orange juice and set out four cups and saucers.

"Wow," Dad says when he comes out to the backyard in his gardening gear. "Now, this is a picnic. Those are some lucky friends you have." He wanders from rosebush to rosebush, checking on each of them while we wait for our friends to arrive. I watch him, waiting for him to notice the new blooms on the Juniper rosebush. He hasn't said anything about it since Baxter pointed it out to me and Naomi at the beginning of the week, so I'm hoping he knows exactly how to fix it.

He pauses when he gets to its spot on the lawn. He leans over it. Crouches down and looks at the roots, looks back and forth from that rosebush to the others. "Huh," he says.

"The rosebush okay?" I ask.

Dad tilts his head, and I can tell he's trying to communicate with the bush. He said once that if you listen, plants tell you what they need. I don't think he meant that they literally speak words to him, but I know he needs quiet to be able to do his work. So I go very quiet.

I know it looks different, but the rosebush looks sort of beautiful too. It looks like all the roses want to be on that one bush, like it's the best bush to hang out on. And I love how big the petals are. How bright too.

"I don't think it needs more water," Dad says. "I—don't know what it needs. Maybe I should pick off some of the flowers? There's a lot of them."

"That's okay, right?" I ask.

"Of course," Dad says. "The soil here is fantastic. It's easy to grow pretty much everything. I'm sure it's just loving Eventown as much as we are."

Before I can ask any more questions, Veena and Betsy bound out to the backyard and Naomi yips with excitement, and Betsy *oohs* and *ahs* over our picnic setup.

"Happy birthday!" they call out in unison, as if they're twins too.

Betsy hands us each a pair of barrettes like the kind she and now Naomi are always wearing. Veena has a fancy mixing bowl for me and a gymnastics figurine for Naomi. For once, the present-getting part doesn't feel as important as the actual party part of our birthday.

We settle onto the picnic blanket, and Naomi hands out Veena's and Betsy's hats. They each clearly fall in love with the oversized brims and good-smelling flowers.

"These are so cool," Veena says.

"Dad made them," I say, not wanting to brag but also wanting them to know that we know our dad is kind of amazing.

"I love the teacups!" Betsy says. They are white with red roses painted on them. Delicate and almost small enough for dolls to use instead of humans.

"Naomi's idea," I say, and Naomi beams at me. Finally, I've said something that she likes.

The girls say hi to Dad, and he sort of covers the rose-bush with his body.

"You have a very nice home," Veena says to Dad, and I can tell it's the kind of super-polite thing her mom reminded her to say. The word *home* gives me a funny pang in my chest.

Juniper felt like home for a long time, but then it

changed because so many other things changed. Eventown doesn't feel like home yet, but I like it here. But if Juniper's not home anymore and Eventown's not home yet, does that mean I don't have a home right now?

My skin aches at the thought. My feet sweat. I shiver my shoulders a little, in the hopes that I can shake it off.

Feel normal, I tell my heart, and it tries to listen, I think.

"We love our new home!" Naomi says.

My stupid heart is making me want to yell at her. *We haven't agreed that this is home! I want to cry. We're not ready! Why are you leaving me behind? You're the worst sister in the world!*

"So, what's being twelve like?" Veena asks. I don't know when she'll turn twelve, but I guess she's still eleven. I'm about to answer, but Betsy butts in.

"It's sort of like you feel calmer," Betsy says. "And I grew an inch on my twelfth birthday. I wonder if you guys grew."

I don't think it's possible that Betsy grew an inch all at once. But I think of the little rosebud that popped up in front of my eyes and change my mind. Maybe it is possible.

"Do people or, like, other things grow more quickly here?" I ask.

"Probably," Betsy says. "Everything's better here."

"Do you think I've grown an inch today?" Naomi asks. She stands up very, very straight and pulls me up to stand back-to-back with her.

I can tell that we are exactly the same height still. We've lined up like this a billion times before.

"I wish I was a twin," Betsy says. It surprises me. I didn't think Betsy thought anything about her life was imperfect.

"It's pretty great," I say.

Naomi nods, but she doesn't say anything.

I tell my heart not to hurt.

Veena's brought something sticky and orange and delicious called jalebi for dessert, and as soon as she brings it out everyone asks her a bunch of questions about it. We all try it at the same time. After a few bites of jalebi, I feel fine again. It tastes a little like fried dough but with more flavor.

"Now, that is a dessert," Dad says. In his voice I hear how bad we all know my last attempt at cake was. I don't feel embarrassed, though. I wait for my heart to flip and my skin to flush, but nothing happens. In fact, when I think about how I normally might be embarrassed about a failed cake, I can't seem to remember if I ever felt embarrassed about one before.

Or the last time I was embarrassed at all.

I can't remember, either, the story I told at the Welcoming Center. My most humiliating moment.

"What kind of dessert did we have at our eleventh birthday?" I ask Naomi. "Do you remember?"

Naomi stuffs more jalebi into her mouth and shrugs.

"The bakery in town makes amazing cakes," Veena

says, and I get the feeling she's trying to change the subject. "Mine was decorated with my face last year. It was sort of creepy, actually. But cool!"

"I got an ice cream cake for my twelfth birthday," Betsy says. "Rose-vanilla. Obviously."

"Oh! Like we had a few weeks ago! That's so funny," I say.

Betsy squints at me like I don't make any sense at all to her.

"I had an ice cream cake one year," I say, "but it melted and I totally freaked out. I was, like, seven, so I freaked out all the time."

Betsy doesn't stop her squinting. "So did you guys go to the Welcoming Center yet?" she asks.

Naomi and I nod.

"Oh, cool!" Veena says. "What was it like?"

Naomi looks at me, and I look back at her. Now would be the moment we could tell Veena and Betsy about getting interrupted by Veena's mom. Now would be the right time to ask why her mom was there, and if it was okay that I didn't finish telling my stories.

But Naomi's face tells me not to say anything. I know the face well. It is her *let us fit in* face, her *don't cause a stir* face.

I give the tiniest nod back. I won't tell Veena if Naomi won't tell our parents.

"Really good cake," Naomi says.

"Yeah, but they should serve jalebi there, instead of cake," I say so that I don't say anything else. Betsy laughs like it's the funniest idea in the world, but I don't see what's so funny. The jalebi makes me feel very welcomed. And I keep discovering new layers of taste. "Does this have lemon? And roses?" I ask.

"Yes! There's lemon juice and my mom dips them in rosewater. I guess it's a family tradition."

"What do you mean? Does your grandmother make jalebi too?" I ask.

Veena shrugs.

"Is she still in India?"

Veena shrugs. I should know enough to stop asking questions, but once they start I can't stop them.

"Do you think you'll visit India someday?"

Naomi nudges me with her foot and Betsy pretends she didn't hear.

Veena finally stops shrugging. She looks right at me, like she's seeing something new on my face—a new constellation of freckles, a new difference between my face and Naomi's.

Naomi changes the subject to Chase, the boy she and Betsy both think is cute, but Veena doesn't take her eyes off me.

"That would be so cool," Veena whispers, under the din of Naomi and Betsy's Chase-chatter.

Then, as if she never said a word, she says something about the color of Chase's eyes and how many times he looked at Naomi in music class, and I wonder if that tiny moment ever happened, and why wanting to go to India someday would ever be a secret.

Betsy asks me who I think is cute, but I don't think any of the boys are cute. I say there was someone in Juniper who I thought was cute, and right away Betsy says she has to go to the bathroom instead of asking me about them. When she's all the way in the house, Veena leans over and motions for us to come closer. We scoot closer on the blanket, our knees touching. Veena whispers.

"Betsy's one of the only other kids in town who wasn't born here," she says. "A lot of our parents were born outside of Eventown. But Betsy's the only kid who came from some other place when she was really little. Since we only take one new family a year, a lot of them are grown-ups or babies, but usually there's not someone our age. And we're not supposed to—talking about other places isn't really—maybe you shouldn't mention Juniper. Even though it sounds really cool. And interesting. But I think the less you talk about it the easier it will be."

"The easier what will be?" I ask.

Betsy comes back before the question gets answered. She

doesn't sit back down. "Veena. We need to go," she says. She sounds like a teacher. A principal, even. Stern. In charge.

"We just got here," Veena says.

"We need to go. Now." Betsy jerks her head toward my dad and the rosebush. Dad is picking roses from the bush, but it doesn't seem to be helping much. It looks incredibly crowded. Somehow, since Veena and Betsy got here, the rosebush looks even more brilliant, bigger, less like everything else around it. And Dad circling it over and over doesn't seem to be making anyone more comfortable.

"It's just a rosebush," I say, so quietly they might not hear me. And maybe Betsy doesn't, but Veena does. Her eyes find mine and her fingers wrap around her necklaces.

"Maybe we can stay . . . ," she says, but Betsy tugs on her arm. I see the exact moment when she gives in to the pull. "Tell your dad to go visit my mom and dad. They'll know how to help," Veena says. "Don't worry. And happy birthday!" They vanish down the road so fast I don't even have time to say thank you.

They've left behind their hats too. The hats look silly, all of a sudden, abandoned in the middle of our yard. They're all wrong for a twelfth birthday.

Naomi glares at me. "You aren't following the rules," she says. "The Welcoming Center. The questions. Even your stupid cake."

"I don't control how roses grow, Naomi," I say. I'm tired

of her giving me this look every time something goes wrong.

"You've been weird since the Welcoming Center," she says. "You've been different."

I shake my head and try to unhear her.

"Dad?" I call out. "What's going on with the roses?"

"I'm sorry, girls. I'm trying to fix it. It's turning out to be a little tricky." He goes inside to find something else to help the rosebush and I lean close to it to see if I can figure out what it needs, why it's already grown higher than it was this morning, why there are so many blooms I can barely see the stems.

Naomi joins me. She doesn't say anything, but she stands so close I can hear her breathing, I can feel her seeing what I'm seeing.

And what I'm seeing is a little strange.

Weeds. Not already grown ones. But brand-new weeds, crowding right around the base of the bush, sprouting and growing and spreading before our eyes.

I reach for Naomi's hand, but she pulls it to her chest and doesn't let me have it. There are only five weeds growing, and they are skinny and almost easy to miss. But the way they grow is so fast, so insistent, so incredibly strange, that I can't tear my eyes away.

I look all around the other yards that I can see from here. I don't see a single weed. I don't see anything else growing like it's in fast-forward.

Baxter is outside doing his homework. He waves and I wave back. Naomi waves, too, but she's focused on the growing weeds.

Lickety-split, she pulls them from the ground and stuffs them in her pockets. She kicks dirt over the places they sprouted from. She stomps her feet into the ground a little, demanding nothing else grow there.

She doesn't look at me or say a word.

She watches the ground another moment, to make sure nothing new grows. Nothing does. Her pockets are full, and Baxter's straining to get a look at what in the world we're doing. But the moment's over before he catches it. As if it never happened at all.

26
Only Three

"Maybe we should tell Veena about the weeds," I say to Naomi when we wake up Monday morning for school. "She said her parents could help." It's been on my mind since Naomi shoved the weeds in her pockets on our birthday. We haven't spoken about them at all. We haven't spoken about our failed birthday party either. Instead we tested each other for our vocabulary quiz, and we went on a hike with Mom and to the market with Dad to pick up more green strawberries and a whole entire pound of maple fudge.

Then we ate so much maple fudge that we should have gotten sick, but instead we just got happy and silly and played a two-person game of tag in the yard as the sun spent hours sinking behind the Eventown Hills.

It was a great weekend, except every once in a while I'd think about the look on Betsy's face when she saw the rosebush, and the abandoned party hats and the sadness of a party that stops before it's supposed to, and the look on Naomi's face when she shoved the weeds into her pockets, and a thousand questions popped into my head.

"Why would we tell Veena?" Naomi asks. "Why do you want to tell Veena every little thing?" She's laid her outfit on the ground, and when she rolls out of bed she puts it on right away like she doesn't want to be seen in the fuzzy yellow pajamas we both have.

"It was weird, don't you think? And Veena sometimes explains stuff when something seems weird."

Naomi's outfit is perfect. Her purple tights match her purple T-shirt and her gray skirt looks pretty with her gray cardigan. I put on flowered leggings and a flowy green top that I tie with a pink belt. It doesn't match, but I think it matches the town—all green and flowery and colorful.

Naomi wrinkles her nose at it.

"Can't you wear something else?" she says. "Those leggings are weird."

I ignore her. Because if I didn't ignore her I might say something mean, like that sometimes I wish she could be different than she is too. Naomi's always wishing I were more like Betsy, I think. And sometimes I'm wishing Naomi could be someone sillier and stronger and nicer to me. Someone who gets why floral leggings and a green top go together better than an all-gray-and-purple outfit. Someone who gets why it doesn't matter if it all matches anyway.

When Naomi turns around, I sneak a look at the photograph of young Dad. For some reason, it makes me feel better.

"Do you think things always grow that way in Eventown?" I ask. I'm not ready to let it go.

"Why are you so obsessed with asking questions that no one wants to answer?" Naomi says. She isn't using an angry voice, but her words are mean. "Why can't you just leave things be?"

"I thought you would be curious too," I say in a small voice.

"I'm curious why you can't just make nice conversation. Or say who you think is cute. Or make a vanilla cake. Or stay quiet in class. Or see how happy Mom and Dad are here and that everything's better and there's no reason to worry about weeds or anything else. You're making something easy so hard. Even a birthday party. Why aren't you happy the way I am? The way Mom and Dad are?"

"I'm happy," I say, but I know I'm not saying it loud enough for her to believe me. "I am mostly really happy," I try again. "And when I'm not happy I try really hard to be happy."

202

There's a grip in my heart, and Naomi's right here but she feels a million miles away, on a whole other planet, and she gets to be there with Mom and Dad and I'm stuck here, on my weird little planet all alone. I want to explain all of that to her, but every time I try to explain what is making me feel unsettled or weird, all I do is get further and further away. My planet keeps getting pushed farther into space, and I have no idea how to leap off it and be on their planet.

Sometimes, the only thing that makes me feel like I'm not all by myself on my weird planet is that photograph of young Dad. Sometimes I pretend I'm in that garden with him, able to be myself without anyone getting mad about it. I want to look at it again, right now.

But mostly I want Naomi to stop saying how different and weird I am.

"I guess I'm not upset," I say. "I guess I'm happy too. I'll forget about the weeds."

Naomi relaxes. "Good," she says. "You should be happy. I'll cook something with you tonight, okay? Or bake something. We can make banana bread. You love making banana bread."

I do. I love making banana bread. "Okay," I say.

"It's going to be a good day," Naomi says. "Any day that Mom makes cinnamon rolls is a good day."

"Even though they'd be better if I made them," I say.

"*Obviously*," Naomi says with a big grin, and I try to make Naomi grinning at me enough to make me grin too.

I am trying so, so hard.

The trying works. Pretty much. We do finger painting in art class, and I thought it was sort of for babies, but it ends up being really fun. I ace our vocabulary quiz, and there's spaghetti and meatballs for lunch. And as if I get a reward for asking zero questions and being quiet about the weeds all day, Naomi asks Veena and Betsy to go to the ice cream shop with us after school.

"Ooooh, today's flavor is chocolate-blueberry," Veena says when we get there. I remember when we were on vacation here, there was a different flavor every day, each more magical than the last.

"I wonder how they come up with so many different kinds," I say. "They have such cool ideas. Will they just try anything?" I'm imagining myself working here over the summer, someday, maybe as Junior Ingredient Decider or Ice Cream Maker in Training.

"What do you mean?" Veena asks. Naomi orders a scoop of chocolate-blueberry for each of us. They come in sugary cones and not a single drop melts off the top.

"The different flavors they have every day. How do they come up with them?" I take a lick of my scoop. It's delicious and delicate and I could eat gallons of it. It's a little familiar on my tongue.

"There's only three," Veena says. "Vanilla-rose, chocolate-blueberry, and maple-caramel."

"Only three?" I ask. I look to Naomi, search her for disappointment or confusion, but it's not there. She's attacking her cone with a closed-eyes contentment I've rarely seen on her face.

"They rotate. One of those three flavors every day. All using the best Eventown ingredients. That's what makes it so delicious. Everything's fresh." Veena laps at her cone, but I don't return to mine.

Still, it doesn't melt. Not even as I wait a full minute, then two, before licking it again. It stays cold and solid and still somehow creamy.

Perfect.

"Oh," I say. "I thought—we all thought—we assumed there was a different flavor every day." I think back to a few weeks ago when we came with Veena, and a few years before that when the whole family came. The shop is as perfect as it was in our memories, but I'm disappointed anyway.

As disappointed as the day we went to the library.

I lick my nonmelting ice cream.

"It's like the library," I say, hoping Veena or at least Naomi will agree with me.

"How is an ice cream shop anything like a library?" Naomi asks. She laughs and Betsy laughs, but I'm not laughing.

"It's . . ." I can't find the words. I know that the Eventown library is different from libraries back home and I know this ice cream place is different from what I thought it was in my mind.

I don't remember all my stories from back home, or even all my feelings, but I remember enough to know that in Juniper we had many kinds of different ice cream flavors and that we had libraries filled with books and that those books were filled with words.

I look at Naomi. I want her to remember all the things I'm remembering. But the look on her face tells me that her memories are even blurrier than mine. That some of them are all the way gone. Maybe she has forgotten all our stories from getting ice cream back home. Maybe she's even forgotten what it was like to read at the library, lying on the blue carpet in between the stacks, flipping pages and laughing or crying at what we found there.

I sort of miss licking ice cream off the side of my hand. I sort of miss worrying that it will drip to the ground, fall apart, melt too fast. I miss the race against time that was getting a cone. I look at Naomi. I want her to miss all that too.

But Naomi is lost in her cone.

I know, the way I sometimes know things about my twin that she doesn't exactly tell me, that Naomi doesn't remember the way melted ice cream used to make rivers on our hands. And she doesn't remember our happiest memories at the Juniper Ice Cream Café.

So I keep those little scenes to myself, like a book no one else has ever read.

And I try to enjoy the ice cream, but the perfect flavor and the way it never melts doesn't make me as happy as the things my heart remembers.

I look at the faces of my sister and friends.

I am starting to think it's possible I am the only person in the whole town who has these sticky, strange, shuddering feelings.

Like the Juniper rosebush, I'm not quite fitting into this new place.

And like the Juniper rosebush, no one understands why.

27

Dandelion Invasion

On Thursday morning I make oatmeal and bacon for everyone and watch the dandelions that have taken over our yard. It is a sea of yellow outside, like the sun has dyed our whole yard with its brightest beams. It would be beautiful if it weren't also a little scary.

"It's a dandelion invasion," Dad says, like we are suddenly at war with our plants.

"People are noticing, Todd," Mom says in a voice that she thinks we can't hear but of course we can.

"Betsy noticed the rosebush," Naomi says.

"Everyone noticed everything," I say, because we have spent three days of school trying to answer the question of

208

why our yard has been looking so strange. Naomi started telling people that Dad was working on special flowers for the center of town, and I guess people believed that. Sort of.

Still, they are looking at us a little funny. In a way that makes me remember being looked at like I'm different, like I'm not the right person to be friends with, like I'm no longer in the club of normal kids with normal families and normal rosebushes.

Naomi is very, very quiet about the whole thing. I can see her brain working, but I can't see what it's thinking.

"It's like Juniper," I say. "I remember sometimes people looking at us like this in Juniper." I can't remember why they looked at us this way, but I remember the way it felt after.

Lonely. So lonely I sometimes crawled under my covers and wouldn't come out. So lonely I wished and wished and wished to be normal again.

"Don't talk about that place," Naomi says, sprinkling extra cinnamon on her perfect bowl of oatmeal. I made it because it's comfort food and I thought we might all need comfort. "We're here now."

"I don't know what that means," I say.

Naomi looks at me funny. Mom does too. Dad only looks out the window. It's going to be a long day. Maybe oatmeal wasn't the right breakfast after all.

A vine winds its way over our window, splitting the morning view in two. We all gasp.

"Todd. Go cut that vine down, please," Mom says. She sounds calm and looks calm, but I know there must be something more underneath all that ease. "This is fine, I'm sure. It's a little odd, but I'm sure there's a perfectly good explanation. There always is. Now, let's not get distracted by these silly weeds. Get yourselves all ready for school, okay?"

Naomi and I nod, and I'm not scared, but I'm something else. I'm full of wondering. And questions. And I know that Eventown doesn't like questions very much.

When we're done brushing teeth and packing bags and shoving our feet inside shoes, we step out on the lawn, backpacks strapped to our backs, and take in the sight. The dandelions are relentless. No other lawns have dandelions. None of them have weeds of any kind. The grass of other lawns is green and short and even. It looks freshly mowed every day.

"You need to go back," Naomi says.

"Go back where? Juniper?"

"No. The Welcoming Center. You need to go back there and finish."

I thought maybe she'd forgotten, or at least finally given up on worrying about it, but it's clear that's one thing she hasn't forgotten. "They haven't said anything about it," I say.

210

I expected Christine and Josiah to stop by or find Mom and tell her to bring me back in. But it seems like they got so distracted by whatever argument they had with Ms. Butra and her friends that they don't remember that I didn't finish telling stories.

"Well, I'm saying something about it," Naomi says. "Don't you think it was weird? Mom and Dad made it seem like the Welcoming Center is a big deal. Betsy too. And if it's a big deal and it didn't go well, doesn't that mean something?"

"There's stuff you haven't wanted to tell people too," I say. "You kept those weeds a secret from Dad, and now look. And I said we should ask Veena about what happened with her mom at the Welcoming Center."

"Veena's not in charge," Naomi says.

"Neither are you," I say.

Naomi crosses her arms. I do the same.

"They'll probably just have you go back and finish. It's not a big deal."

I think about the three stories I didn't tell. My angriest time, my loneliest time, my most joyful time. They're still clear in my head. I can turn them upside down and around and dream about them at night. The memories I did tell are gone. I can't reach them. And I don't want to make these last three vanish too.

"I'm not going back," I say. I know before I say the words that Naomi won't like them. That even worse, she won't understand them.

"Yes, you are. You will after I tell Mom and Dad," Naomi says. She looks the way she does when she's called on in class and knows the answer but doesn't want to say it because she hates speaking in front of everyone.

Sometimes I would jump in and answer for her. I'd get in trouble, but it was always worth it, for the way that she relaxed and smiled her sister-smile at me.

Now, though, Naomi won't protect me the way I've always protected her.

"The stories I told them are gone," I say. "I don't want to let go of my happiest story."

"Your happiest story will be one you have here, in Eventown," Naomi says. "How could anything be happier than here?" She's getting exasperated, her voice tired and urgent. *Why won't you agree with me already?* the words under her words say.

I don't know how to answer, because the happy story is so simple I think Naomi wouldn't understand it. The memory is of the house smelling like a jasmine–olive oil cake with white chocolate–pear frosting and being awake when everyone else in the house was asleep. It was knowing everyone in the family was happy and full because of me.

212

It was realizing I wasn't worried about anything and it was sneaking downstairs for one more piece of cake and putting a Beatles record on Mom's record player with the volume turned way down low.

I know without telling her that Naomi won't understand any of that right now.

I know without telling her that Naomi probably doesn't remember any of those things. The smell of the cake or the sound of the music or the way it felt to be in the house in Juniper on a night when nothing had gone wrong. There were lots of sad nights in Juniper, so the ones that were happy were like finding buried treasure.

I want to hold on to the map that leads me to those memories, to that treasure.

"I'm not ready to let go of all my stories," I say, hoping if I say it with the right tone, with the right combination of words, Naomi will understand. But she doesn't hear me. She sighs and, I think, wishes I were more like Betsy and less like Elodee.

She starts the walk to school, but I linger on the lawn for a moment longer and watch the vines continue to grow, covering more and more of our house.

I swear I can hear the rosebush growing another inch and more dandelions poke through the ground, brushing up against my sandaled toes.

Inside, I'm sure, the kitchen still smells like bacon and warm cinnamon and the best kind of home.

But outside.

Outside something is happening.

28
Twinness

There are whispers at school. The whispers are about us. I know, because I hear the words *twins* and *new* and *weeds* and *roses*. I hear the words *different* and *strange* and *stay away*.

They have seen our house. Maybe not all of them, but the ones who haven't seen it have heard about it. Juniper was a small town, and Eventown is an even smaller town. And in a tiny town, it's impossible to hide the things you hope no one notices.

People notice.

I remember from Juniper the way it feels to walk down the halls with people talking about me, but I don't remember why they ever talked about us before. And not knowing the why makes the feeling stranger, wilder, more like the vines and the dandelions and the rosebush.

Naomi waves at Betsy and she waves back, but weakly. She looks almost sad. I didn't know Betsy ever looked sad.

"Do you remember making people sad, in Juniper?" I ask my sister.

"Elodee. Please stop asking what I remember," she says with a sigh as big as a stormy wind. "I don't remember anything that you're talking about. I remember a stupid white house and a crowded school bus and Dad working on the garden just like he does here, and you baking and cooking all the time just like you do here. And I remember the gym and the creaky beam and wanting to go to the mall all the time. That's pretty much it. That was our life there. The end."

"That's not the end," I say. "There's more to remember." I tell myself to stop talking, stop asking her questions, but I can't. I need a teammate. I need her to feel what I'm feeling and remember what I'm feeling and not leave me out here by myself with the whispers and the wondering.

"Not for me," Naomi says. Naomi wants out of this conversation. I can tell from the way she keeps looking over my shoulder, from the way her toes and elbows point away from me, her whole body practically twisting itself away from me. "We have everything we need here. The story of the day we ate the best ice cream. The story of the day a butterfly landed on my shoulder. The story of the day I fell in love with playing the cymbals. The story of the day we first ate jalebi. What else could you possibly want?"

I try to feel the same way Naomi does. I try to make those stories feel like enough. I stare really hard at all the things that are the same about us. Our hair, our eyes, our noses, our chins. It's not enough.

Naomi runs ahead to get into class and I follow behind, taking tiny steps.

I get to my seat right when Ms. Applebet is taking attendance and everyone's eyes are all over me when I raise my hand to say I'm here. Math class starts, and I can't pay any attention to numbers and the ways they pile on top of each other and divide themselves up.

Veena passes me a note.

It's okay, it reads.

I don't understand, I write back. Veena takes her time writing me back. She pretends to consider long division, but I know she's thinking through how to explain Eventown to me. She'll scribble something down, then stick her tongue out of the side of her mouth a little, erase it, and write something else.

Naomi keeps glancing over at me, to make sure I'm

not being weird, I think. Betsy doesn't look my way. Other people are passing notes, and I feel like they must be about my family, but I try to focus on Veena's fast-writing hand and nothing else. Definitely not long division or the fact that I suddenly notice Naomi and Betsy are wearing the same outfit—red skirts, gray T-shirts, black Mary Janes, shiny black rhinestone barrettes in their hair.

Twins.

Veena has to poke my arm to get my attention because my eyes are busy looking back and forth between Naomi and Betsy, checking out every new similarity. Each one breaks my heart a little. *SHE'S MY TWIN, NOT YOURS!* I want to yell.

But that would only make me weirder, and it would make Naomi more upset with me, and it would make me even lonelier.

So I swallow it all down and shiver a little from how big and pulsing those feelings are, and I open Veena's note.

The houses here are like you and Naomi—twins. Imagine if Naomi's hair turned blue and your eyes got bigger and Naomi's nose shrank down to a little button nose and your chin got all pointy. You'd be scared, right? Because you're used to being the same. It's like that here. Your lawn isn't the same anymore. And no one knows why. But it has to mean something is wrong. If Naomi suddenly wasn't your twin, it would mean something's wrong, right?

I read Veena's note three times. Then three more.

Naomi has my eyes and hair and chin still. We're the same height and have the same hands, and anyone passing us on the street would still smile at our twinness.

But.

But. So much else isn't the same. And so much never was the same. And Veena's right. It makes me feel weird, to see the differences, to have to live with them.

I understand, I write back. And I almost pass it to her with nothing else, but I think about our lawn, and yes, it's strange and different and a little frightening to some people, but the shock of yellow dandelions was exciting too. Can't something be both unsettling or scary and beautiful? I write more after a lot of thinking about not-math,

I wish everyone loved seeing an enormous rosebush, because it's pretty. And seeing plants grow in front of your eyes is cool too. I mean, it's sort of scary. I get it. But back home everyone would think the big roses were the best ones.

I watch Veena read my note. She gives me a sad smile and writes one last note. This time, she just holds it up in front of her face so I can see it.

You're not back home, though.

29
A Little Bit of Saltiness

"Betsy's going to come to my gymnastics meet today," Naomi says after school. "You don't have to."

"Oh," I say. "I want to." Naomi looks everywhere but at my face. "Unless you don't want me to?"

"Maybe not today," she says at last. "I bet you want to do something else anyway. Bake or something."

"You don't want me there," I say. It isn't a question, so I don't phrase it like one.

She doesn't want to say it. Saying it will change everything. So instead Naomi adjusts her skirt, which matches Betsy's skirt. I raise my eyebrows. "You have a new twin now," I say.

Naomi rolls her eyes. "It's for fun."

"You've never wanted to dress like me," I say. It's true. Even back in Juniper I'd sometimes want us to dress the same and confuse our friends, and Naomi always wrinkled her nose and said no, that it would be weird.

"I don't know what you're talking about," she says. "You're being weird. We'll hang out tonight, okay? Look at the stars and eat cookies? Maybe tell Mom and Dad about the Welcoming Center thing and you needing to go back? Then you can come to my next meet."

I don't want to watch the stars and eat cookies in our wild garden of a yard. And I definitely don't want to tell Mom and Dad or talk about telling them anymore.

I nod anyway. Naomi won't listen to all the other words I want to say.

Besides, I don't need to watch her do the same gymnastics routine as every other girl on her team. There's nothing exciting about that. There's nothing stressful or joyful or heart-thumping about it. She'll be perfect, they'll be perfect, and no one will win or lose.

I won't be missing much at all.

Veena skips the gymnastics meet with me and invites me over to her house, so I go. Ms. Butra greets us at the door with jalebi. We devour three pieces each before even saying hello. That's how good jalebi is.

"This is amazing," I say.

Ms. Butra smiles. "Veena says you love cooking too."

I nod. "It's easier here," I say. I wait for some sign from Ms. Butra, some indication that she understands what I'm saying.

"That's true," she says. "Certain things are very easy to cook here. But not everything."

"It took my mom years to make jalebi here," Veena explains.

"And it's still not right," Ms. Butra says. She has a sort of funny look on her face, like she's remembering something. It makes my heart leap. No one here ever looks like they're remembering anything at all. Ms. Butra squints at me, like she's looking for the answers to how to make the perfect jalebi, but I have no idea of course. "Has that happened to you here?"

I nod, thinking of my cake. Veena nods, too, remembering our afternoon together.

"Cooking and baking certain things comes from the stories of our lives—recipes passed down from generations before, or things we made when we were celebrating a certain occasion or feeling down about something or spending time with a favorite person. I made jalebi back in India. And I don't remember much about India. Not much at all."

Ms. Butra is speaking in a soft voice and I know from the way she's choosing her words that she's telling me a secret. She's saying things to me she doesn't say to everyone. "Do you remember much from your life before Eventown?" she asks, and I know it's a big question.

It might even be a dangerous question.

I nod.

"If you can even remember a little, you can start to bake the things you want to bake. I remembered rose water and getting a squeeze of lemon in my eyes and someone's hands that were darker than mine and more wrinkled. That was almost enough to make the jalebi the way I wanted to."

"But not quite enough," I say.

"No," Ms. Butra says. "Not quite."

"Elodee tried to make a special cake," Veena says.

"A special cake," Ms. Butra says, like it's the most wonderful thing she's ever heard. "Well, maybe I can help. Let's make a cake."

"Right now?" I ask.

"I don't see why not," Ms. Butra says. "What kind of cake are we making?"

For a moment I feel nervous to tell her. But I trust Ms. Butra and her jalebi. "Jasmine–olive oil cake with white chocolate–pear frosting," I say, wanting her to taste the words in her mouth, the way I do.

Ms. Butra grins. "I knew I liked you," she says. "Let's get to work."

* * *

Ms. Butra's kitchen is chock-full of ingredients, but she sends Veena's dad out for jasmine and pears.

"Now," she says before we begin. "Don't tell me the stories you remember, but hold them in your mind and maybe something will come to you. And if it doesn't, that's okay too. We'll do the best we can. It's going to take time to find the taste you want."

I close my eyes. Like Ms. Butra, I see hands—bigger than mine but not too big. I hear music playing in the background, but I know we can't play any here, so that won't help. I see eyes that are blue like mine but darker. And I see a tiny green bowl of sea salt on the counter.

"Sea salt," I say. "For the pears, I think. They need sea salt."

"Wonderful," Ms. Butra says. "One ingredient at a time."

We start baking. This time I bake the pears instead of putting them on the stovetop, and I sprinkle sea salt on top. I mix a little salt into the cake mixture as well and go easier on the olive oil. We try to make a jasmine jam and a jasmine powder and a jasmine broth, but none of it is quite right.

We try adding other spices to jasmine, and I like the way it smells mixed with thyme, so we go with that.

Ms. Butra is confident in the kitchen. She handles everything gently, and I try to imitate the way she stirs, the way she chops, even the face she makes when she tastes a little bit from a bowl or pan.

At some point she notices me watching her. "You've got your own special way in the kitchen," she says. "Do it your own way."

Veena overhears and smiles at me. We all do it our own way, and when we mix the flavors we each taste it and add new things to the mix. Same with the frosting. We play and experiment and talk about what very, very little I can remember about making the cake before, and soon it's ready for the oven.

I know it won't be right. But I also know it will be better than before.

We paint watercolors of cake while we wait for it to come out of the oven, and Ms. Butra looks through the necklaces on Veena's neck. She gives me one with a birthday cake charm.

"Maybe this will help you remember," she whispers into my ear. "You never know."

"I thought I'm not supposed to—"

"Some of us don't agree," she says. I wait for her to say more, but she doesn't.

When the cake comes out of the oven, it doesn't taste right. It's sweet in the wrong places and the frosting isn't thick enough and thyme was the wrong herb for sure.

But the sea salt. The sea salt is right. That little bit of saltiness reminds me of a checkered apron and oven mitts shaped like ducks and the way it felt to peek in the oven when the cake wasn't done yet, to see if I could watch it turn from batter into something delicious.

It tastes terrible, mostly.

But good, too, for the way it reminds me of before.

Good, for how wrong it is. How imperfect.

How uneven.

30
The Vines

We don't wake up Friday morning the way we usually would—by light streaming in our windows and welcoming us into the day.

We don't wake up that way because no light streams in. We wake up to Mom and Dad bursting through our door. They are both in pajamas with messy hair and startled faces. There is no smell of bacon or French toast or even roses. Something is blocking out the Eventown smell.

"It's ten!" Mom says. "It's ten and it's dark in here and the windows are completely covered. Completely, completely covered." Mom's voice is funny, like it's been flattened by a very heavy object. I think it's how surprise sounds here in Eventown.

"What are you saying about windows?" Naomi asks groggily, but I think I already know. I can feel the way things are shifting, the way I used to be able to tell if it was going to rain, back when we lived somewhere with rain.

"The vines," Mom says.

"They've grown over the windows," Dad says. "They're quite persistent. They're sort of, well, taking over a little. I can't quite seem to figure out what to do about it. I had to cut through the ones covering the doorway just to get outside this morning." He looks disappointed in himself, like he's supposed to know, like maybe he isn't such a great gardener after all.

I hold his hand and hope that makes the feeling dull.

Mom leads us all outside so that we can look at the house. My stomach is rumbling, asking for food, and a part of me doesn't want to see the way things are changing. Naomi keeps glaring at me.

"What?" I whisper.

"Things are getting weirder," she whispers back.

"I can see that."

"Things started getting ruined after the Welcoming Center. I keep trying to tell you that."

"Oh my god, you're obsessed," I say, but when I think

about it, I think she could be right. Everything was predictable and normal and perfect until that strange, imperfect, unpredictable moment when my Welcoming got interrupted.

"Don't you think we should go back to the Center? Just in case?" Naomi says. Her whisper is urgent now. "Maybe we should tell Mom and Dad and see what they think. I bet they'll say you should go back."

"What if this isn't so awful?" I say. "What if this isn't everything getting ruined?"

We both look up at the house and down at the yard.

It doesn't look very ruined to me.

Because everything is growing.

Not growing. Exploding into being.

The roses are now as big as my head.

The bushes are the size of cars, but no one here knows much about cars.

And the vines. The vines are crawling all over every inch of our house now. Covering the windows. Wrapping us up in green and wildness and newness.

I can't help but smile. It's beautiful. Bright and strange and magical, too. But no one else is smiling. Not Mom, who looks off into the distance; not Dad, who frowns at the roots, at the leaves, at the whole garden; and not Naomi, who is nudging me with her elbow, which feels sharper than ever.

"I'm scared," she says. "I'm scared it's our fault, somehow. We're the new people. We're the difference."

I nod. I know that feeling. Sometimes it seems like almost anything could be my fault. The thought, the vines, and Naomi's face make me tired. She's never going to see the chaos on our front lawn as beautiful. I don't think Mom and Dad will either.

I give up.

"Okay," I say. "Okay, fine."

Naomi's shoulders relax. Keeping a secret has been hurting her more than I thought.

"Mom?" she says. "Dad?"

They turn to her.

"Elodee has something to tell you. Something about the day we went to the Welcoming Center."

"You tell them," I mumble.

Naomi takes a deep breath, looking at the vines and the rosebush.

She looks very hard at the rosebush. I wonder what she's looking for, why she seems to be lost in its branches and petals for a moment. But then the moment is gone, and she lifts her chin. "Elodee didn't tell all six stories," she says. "The day we were welcomed, her time was interrupted. She didn't finish. So she has three stories left. Big ones. Stories she was supposed to give away. She's holding on to them."

Naomi's words are completely right. I am holding on hard to my stories. I don't want to give them away. I don't want to lose them.

I'm even a little bit happy that something prevented me from doing the thing I was supposed to do. The thing everyone who lives here does. The thing, I guess, that would have helped us fit in.

What was an accident is starting to feel like something bigger. Something *more*. I'm different from Naomi. I've been feeling different from her. And maybe this is why.

Maybe my stories, my memories, are bigger than I thought.

"Elodee?" Mom says. "Is that true?" I nod. I don't know what to say. Aren't they mine, the stories? Aren't they mine to tell or not tell, to let go of or to hold on to forever?

Dad looks at me with a different look than Mom.

I can't place it at first.

It's not a frown or a smile. There's a crinkle in his eyes that isn't exactly a sparkle but is maybe a glint. A warmth. A brightness.

It's the look he got once when he thought Naomi was hurt after a meet, but she popped back up and stuck her hands in the air and grinned at the judges. The edges of the memory aren't clear. I can't remember who I was there with or what her routine was or even what the gym looked like or what apparatus she was on. But I remember the joy of her being okay.

It's the look he got when there had been a threat at our school and he came to pick us up to find out that it had all been a prank.

It's the look he got when the rosebush first blossomed.

The look he got when we entered Eventown, when we crossed the border and saw the trees and smelled the pine and blueberries and roses.

Relief. It's the look of relief.

No one else has that look. Maggie and Victor and Baxter on the other side of the house are out on their lawn, frowning. Across the street people have their hands over their mouths, their eyes wide. But here on our lawn, Dad is relieved that I remember some things. He's glad I didn't let go.

The weeds inch from our lawn to Maggie and Victor's.

And right then, as the weeds and vines and roses reach out to new places, find their way to the street, introduce themselves to our neighbors, it starts to rain.

31

Thunder and Lightning

The first drop of rain hits Naomi. I'm sure it's the first drop because she feels it a full ten seconds before anyone else reacts at all. The drop hits her square on the nose, and her voice breaks out louder than it's ever been.

"Oh!"

"What?" I ask.

"I think it might be rain?" she says. "Somehow?"

I remember a hundred stories of playing in the rain with Naomi. Me with an umbrella and her without. Me in a raincoat and her bare-armed. "You love rain," I say.

Naomi looks at the sky, waiting for another drop. I think she almost remembers. I think she almost takes a tiny step closer to me and away from a perfect girl who belongs in Eventown. I think she is almost a girl from far away with knotted wet hair and a cackling laugh and feet that stomp in puddles so hard that the water hits other people in the face. I think she is almost Naomi who loves the rain and doesn't care who knows it.

"I did," Naomi says now, the memory somewhere in her brain still too. "I did love the rain, didn't I?" She looks genuinely confused, stuck between the remembered love and the empty blank space of lost memories, things she must have said in the Welcoming Center or things that were lost because of the spreading, waterlogged forgetting that happens after.

"Maybe you still do," I say, and I hold my hand out to catch the next drop for her, but instead it hits Baxter. He jumps and looks around, as if there's someone doing it to him, instead of it coming from the sky.

"It's cold!" he says. "It's cold water!"

"Don't worry," I call out to him. But Baxter only looks back at me with disgust. He shakes his head. Wipes the raindrop from his forehead. He whispers something to his mother that makes her nod gravely. I am positive that whatever he's said is mean. I didn't know people were ever mean here in Eventown, but I recognize the looks they give us and the way they make me feel.

The last solo drop lands on the rosebush, and it responds as if it's been thirsty its whole life. It shoots up an entire six inches and three more head-sized roses bloom.

More flowers are growing too. Not only roses. Daisies. Tulips. A sunflower is making its way up the side of our house. A patch of pansies is erupting by Baxter's feet. Across the street, a few lilies are coming in. The rain is unearthing a whole garden of new flowers, and I love it for an instant before I remember how much our neighbors hate it.

The rain rushes down, going from one drop at a time to an entire storm in what feels like only seconds.

"Rain," Dad says, like the memory of it is almost but not quite there for him.

"It doesn't rain here," Mom says, trying to understand both the truth of that sentence and the truth of her now-soaking hair all at the same time.

More neighbors rush onto the streets. They are drenched almost instantly, the rain so wrong for Eventown not just because it's falling at all but because of its intensity. It pounds hard, so hard it hurts my eyes, and I huddle close to Naomi because when things are turning entirely upside down I don't know what else to do.

Soon, too soon, there are twenty people on the street, and they are rushing into our yard.

Then there are thirty.

The water rushes the streets, drowns the plants, and the sloshing sound brings back more memories. Naomi and me in matching pink galoshes. An older boy with long legs, like Baxter but not, helping us gather rain in a bucket for a magical potion. An afternoon spent inside, painting rainstorms on poster board with finger paint and glitter while the world got wetter. Three sets of kid-legs splashing in puddles, with Naomi's splashes the most excited, the fastest, the loudest.

I want to tell the crowd all these happy moments, everything rain brings—wet hair and wet socks and cozy days and Naomi's delighted smile and even maybe the bad things, like angry moms who get caught with bags of groceries in a downpour or cars having to move more slowly or ruining your new sweater because it gets all stretched out from the storm. A canceled birthday picnic. Thunderstorms so windy they knock out electricity. Slipping and falling in wet grass, getting your pants all muddy.

But instead we are all in silence on our yard. The town is gathering here, in front of our house and our rosebush and our confused faces, as if somehow we know why rain has come to Eventown today.

Veena and her mom and dad join Naomi and me. Betsy and her moms keep their distance with a group of angry-faced neighbors.

"It's like science class," Veena says. "We learned about this last year. Will we see the big flash of light in the sky soon?"

"Lightning," I say.

"Yes! Lightning! And the other one? The noise?"

"Thunder," Naomi says. Naomi loved thunder best.

Someone, some person I think we loved, called us Thunder and Lightning sometimes. Naomi got Thunder because she loved it and because when she stuck a landing in gymnastics she was met with thunderous applause. I was Lightning because, this person said, I wasn't afraid of being seen.

"Do you remember Thunder and Lightning?" I whisper to Naomi.

She doesn't answer.

Soon there are fifty Eventown residents crowded around our house, and still no one has said a word. They watch in awe; they shake their heads; they sigh and screech and look at each other, waiting for someone to do something, but no one has any idea what to do.

I am maybe the only person in the whole town who truly remembers rain.

There is a flash of lightning in the sky. Bright and brilliant and unmistakable.

My heart jumps. I still feel like that lightning.

Unmissable, not like anyone else, too bright, all wrong for the sky, all wrong for the town.

Something to fear.

The lightning makes the whole town scream in terror. They rush into homes, but not ours.

Veena and her mom stay in our yard.

Betsy and her moms do too.

"What have you done?" Betsy's tall mom says to Mom and Dad. "What are you doing to our town?"

"We don't know anything about this," Mom says. Her voice shakes, though. She remembers what Naomi told her. I can see the possibility shadow her face. She knows something strange *did* happen in our Welcoming. She knows we might not be 100 percent normal.

She stands in front of me, shifting ever so slightly to protect me. I wonder all of a sudden if my difference is visible on my skin, in my eyes, on my face somewhere.

Dad bows his head. He swallows and says nothing.

"You're holding on to your past," Betsy's blue-eyed mom says. "We've seen it before. Not like this. Never like this. But some people"—she looks at Veena's mother and Veena's necklaces—"hold on. Some people think they can have a fresh start while still holding on to their past. But it doesn't work like that. You can be here, or you can be out there. But you can't have both."

239

Betsy's blue-eyed mom sounds like she's speaking in code, but Mom and Dad seem to understand. They nod gravely.

"We want a fresh start," Mom says.

"Do you?" Betsy's tall mom says.

I wish I could decode the conversation better, but the words are as blurry and hazy as some of my memories of life before Eventown.

Veena's mother puts an arm around me and another around Naomi. Veena straightens her back and bites her bottom lip.

Betsy cowers in the rain, shivering and waiting, I think, for another terrifying bolt of lightning.

"Christine and Josiah will be by later today," Betsy's tall mom says. "I'll make sure of it."

She looks right at me, like she knows the secret stories I didn't tell, the stories I want to hang on to, even though, I guess, I'm not supposed to hang on to anything at all.

"I'm sure you will," Ms. Butra says.

"They're kids," Mr. Butra says. I haven't heard him say much of anything before. Veena's dad is usually just quiet and calm. He looks different in the rain. "Kids this age don't come here very often. Asking them to give up so much at their age seems complicated at best."

"It's not giving up," Betsy's tall mom says, rolling her eyes. "It's gaining. Gaining a new life."

"And losing an old one," Ms. Butra says. Her husband nods.

I find myself nodding, too, even though I don't totally understand.

With a sigh and an eye roll, Betsy and her moms decide they are done with the conversation and leave, but the things they've said stay. We all head inside: Veena and her mother and father, Naomi and me and Mom and Dad. Mom makes hot cocoa and Dad offers thick blankets to everyone's shivering shoulders. Mom closes the curtains, tired, I guess, of looking at the storm.

We can still hear it, though. The rain. And sometimes the thunder.

We can see the lightning.

There's no stopping it.

32

Homemade Umbrellas

It rains all weekend.

We are quiet inside our vine-covered home. No one comes to speak to us. The Butras ask if we'd like to come over to their house, where it's less hectic, but Mom says we're fine, this is fine, the Butras don't need to worry about us.

"But I am worried about you," Ms. Butra says. Mom smiles and shakes her head at the very idea.

"We're all in this together," Mom says. "The rain will stop. The plants will stop growing. Everything will be fine. It has to be, doesn't it?"

Ms. Butra doesn't answer.

Christine and Josiah don't come by even though I'm sure

by now Betsy's moms have reported us to them. By now they have remembered that I wasn't properly welcomed. By now, I'm sure, they have come up with a plan to deal with me and my untold stories.

It seems like Naomi and I should come up with a plan, too, but we don't have one.

It feels like we are waiting for something to happen, but nothing happens. We don't do much. I make rainy-day foods like pot roast and grilled cheese and three different kinds of soup and warm chocolate cake and the most delicious chili any of us has ever eaten. Naomi paints pictures of regular-sized roses. I paint the rain and Mom asks me to please throw the paintings away.

Mom has never asked me to throw a painting away before. I've forgotten a lot, but I am almost positive I would remember that.

We wait and wait and the rain doesn't stop and no one knocks at the door and it feels like the house is shrinking or maybe the world is growing. Or maybe that's just how it feels when vines and flowers are flooding your town.

On Monday the rain still hasn't stopped.

Mom has fashioned an umbrella out of a broomstick and a garbage bag and she says she'll walk us to school *just in case*.

"In case of what?" I ask.

"Don't you think you've asked enough questions?" Naomi says, and the words are mean. We are all on edge in the rain. I want to fix it, but I don't know how. So I say mean words back.

"Do you think *you've* asked enough questions?" I say.

"Girls. Can you please try to get along? Please? For your father and me?" We look for Dad, but he's been in the yard all weekend, pulling out weeds that just grow back.

I don't think I've asked enough questions at all, but I don't want Mom and Naomi to keep giving me the looks they're giving me, so I stay quiet.

"And Elodee," Mom says, "we'll be going back to the Welcoming Center tomorrow."

I knew it was coming, but it still makes my breath stop.

"I don't really want to," I say. Naomi huffs. Mom closes her eyes for a moment like she needs to gather all her strength to have this conversation with me.

"I think when you get there, you'll be happy," she says at last, and Naomi nods and the flowers outside keep growing and the rain pounds and pounds and pounds on the roof.

I don't have anything to say to that, so I stay quiet.

Everyone in Eventown is walking to school with their parents. Some of them have homemade umbrellas like ours.

Some have wrapped themselves in plastic wrap or hold buckets and pots and pans and big mixing bowls over their heads. I think some of them must have been in rainstorms long ago, before moving here, but I don't think anyone really remembers the way it feels or that it's not dangerous or bad. I don't think anyone but me remembers splashing and playing and the way puddles are actually pools of pure joy.

We all get to the doors of the school around the same time, and for the first time ever, the parents go in with us, like they are going to start attending school too. Like Mom's about to take a math quiz or Ms. Butra is going to turn in her vocabulary homework.

"Everyone to the music room," Mr. Fountain says, greeting us at the door with a somber look on his face. I wonder if he's spent the morning playing "The Eventown Anthem" on his violin or maybe, just maybe, hearing the music of the raindrops and composing an entirely new anthem from that sound.

I wish that were true, but I know it's not.

We settle in the music room—all the parents, all the kids, Mr. Fountain, Ms. Applebet, Christine, Josiah, and other teachers from other grades who I've seen around school, usually smiling and humming and handing out compliments about someone's dress or hair or latest paper.

Christine and Josiah are clearly the ones in charge. They look over all of us—our wet hair, our disheveled clothes, our makeshift umbrellas, our collection of buckets and trash bags. We do not look the way people in Eventown look. We don't even look the way people in Juniper usually look. We are all one big mess.

"We are going to return to our regular schedules," Christine starts instead of saying hello or welcome or anything a person would normally start with. "But we wanted to check in and let you all know that we are working on the situation, and it should be resolved shortly. Meanwhile, this is a wonderful opportunity for all of us to learn a little about our history, and where we came from."

"The hurricane!" a boy from our grade calls out.

"Yes," Josiah says. "Exactly. This isn't a hurricane. But it's a good example of the way weather can impact a community. A good reminder of why we left places with bad weather. Of why we are all here, and what we gain by living in Eventown."

A roomful of people nods.

"We will be meeting with each family in the next few weeks to make sure Eventown is still the right fit for everyone here," Christine says.

They look extra-long at me and my family before Josiah picks up where Christine left off.

"In the storm that brought Jasper Plimmswood here, so much was lost. This storm, our storm, will not destroy anything. Especially not our town and the way things work here. On that we want to be clear." Josiah's voice is warm and fills up the room. "We will make Jasper Plimmswood proud. And when the storm is over, we will have a fresh start. As always."

A roomful of people nods, again.

"This is the first rain in Eventown," Christine says. "And it is also the last. Of that we can be sure."

Everyone nods once more. But I don't nod and Veena doesn't nod.

Eventown has a plan. Our not-nodding means that we have to have a different plan.

33
The Sky Cries Too

We are at the window watching the rain fall. It's recess time, but we can't go out for recess, so most everyone is painting watercolors of what they would be doing at recess if it were a regular sunny day, but Veena, Naomi, and I are at the window watching the storm. I can't get Christine and Josiah's certainty out of my head. Or the way everyone nodded. Or the way they looked at me, like having memories was the worst thing a person could do.

Most everyone seems miserable about the rain. But I think I see something else on Naomi.

Maybe, if you love something enough, being near it can change everything.

Maybe, if you love something enough, it matters more than fitting in and belonging and being safe.

I think I can almost see Naomi loving the rain again. I can very nearly see her wishing she were in it right now. I'm careful, though. I don't ask her if she remembers this storm or that one. Instead, I try to let her realize herself how pretty the sound of raindrops is. I try to let her remember, the way I remembered adding sea salt to baked pears.

She doesn't have to remember everything. She only has to remember this one thing, I think.

"We need them back," I say.

"Need what back?" Naomi asks. Veena doesn't ask. I think she already knows.

"The stories," I say.

There is a pause like the eye of a storm. Maybe it is the eye of this actual storm, the Eventown Storm, one that might be taught in Eventown history classes in fifty years.

"I don't know what that means," Naomi says. But I think she does know what it means, because she looks scared.

"Once upon a time," I say, quietly so that no one else in class can listen in, "there was a girl named Elodee and another girl named Naomi, and they looked exactly the same, but otherwise they were completely different."

"What are you doing?" Naomi interrupts, but Veena only leans in to hear better.

"I'm telling you a story. A story you probably told them or a story that's connected to a story you told them. A story you can't remember. A story I do remember because I didn't give it away."

Naomi looks like she's about to argue with me, but she seems to change her mind somewhere in between a thought and a word. She sits back.

"Elodee loved the sun," I say. I want to find the perfect words. I speak extra slowly, to make sure they come out right. "She loved sitting in it and running underneath it and watching it move from one side of the sky to another."

"Everyone loves the sun," Naomi says. But she doesn't sound so sure.

"That's what Elodee thought too!" I go on. "But Naomi was different. She loved the rain. She actually loved it so much that during one super-big storm, in the middle of the night, she snuck downstairs into the rain. No one heard her. No one but Elodee."

Veena and Naomi both giggle a little. It's funny to speak in the third person about myself. I let myself smile too.

"Elodee was really, really special. She always knew exactly where her sister was."

"I bet Naomi had that same special skill," Naomi says, smirking a little.

"Maybe," I say.

Ms. Applebet wanders over to us, interrupting my story.

"Girls? You don't want to paint?" she asks. We shake our heads fast, even Naomi. "Hm. Well. Maybe you'd like to step away from the window? I was thinking of closing the blinds. Let everyone get a break from that awful rain." She whispers *rain* like it's a bad word.

"We don't mind the rain," I say. Naomi blushes and Veena looks nervous, but neither of them disagrees with me. We're getting braver, the three of us. Maybe.

"Well," Ms. Applebet says. "Well." She doesn't seem to know how to finish the sentence, so she leaves it be and walks to the other side of the room.

We turn back to the window. The rain is making moving patterns on it, little dances of drops and streaks. I wouldn't mind watching it for one hundred recesses.

"Keep going," Veena says. "I like this story."

"Yeah," Naomi says. "Keep going." I could hug my sister for wanting to hear more, for not wanting to run away from one of my stories of the life we used to have. So I keep going.

"Well. So. Elodee's special skill told her that her sister was outside in the rain. And sure enough, when she looked out their bedroom window, there she was. Her twin sister, all wet and ridiculous, running around in a rainstorm. Elodee knew their mother and father would try to get Naomi out of the rain. They would tell her to come inside. So

Elodee snuck downstairs, as quiet as could be, grabbed an umbrella, and met her sister outside."

Naomi smiles. Maybe, just maybe, she remembers.

"Naomi and Elodee had been having a hard time lately," I say. My voice hitches, but I don't know exactly why. "A very hard time."

It's Veena who interrupts the story now. "Why?" she asks.

I look at Naomi and Naomi looks right back at me. The answer isn't there.

"I don't know," I say, and the not-knowing twists my insides a little. "I don't remember." Naomi bows her head, not remembering either, I'm sure. But we both know we should remember.

"Oh," Veena says. "Okay."

"So," I continue on with the story, hoping maybe an answer will appear—maybe I'll know why the Naomi and Elodee of the story were sad that day, that month, maybe even that whole year. "Naomi and Elodee had been sad for what felt like forever, but this night the sadness was a little further away. Maybe because of the rain."

"Probably because of the rain," Naomi says. It's there, on her face. It's shining in her eyes. The way she loves the rain, the way it matters, loving something imperfect that other people don't understand.

It's all right there on her face: her Naomi-ness.

I've been missing it.

"And when Elodee stepped outside, the rain was warmer than she'd thought it would be. Nicer. Gentler. And Naomi was laughing. Elodee thought she'd never been so happy to see her sister laugh.

"'What are you laughing at?' she asked Naomi.

"'Sometimes the sky cries too,' Naomi said. She looked a little amazed and a little overwhelmed and a little relieved.

Naomi's face shifts again. Her eyes fill up. The way they did that night. The way they did a hundred times or a thousand, before Eventown.

It's hard to keep telling the story, but I want to get it all out, in case it vanishes.

"Elodee laughed with her," I say, my voice a little shaky. "At the rain, at the sky crying, at the way it felt to be in her pajamas in the middle of a storm.

"'Drop your umbrella,' Naomi said, and Elodee did. Elodee was usually the one who bossed Naomi around. Elodee was usually the one to do weird things. But this time, Naomi was the weird one."

Naomi smiles. She doesn't disagree. So I go on. "Naomi handed Elodee a bucket.

"'I'm collecting rain,' Naomi said. Elodee knew what to do. They had collected rain before. It had been a while, though. And it wasn't the same as it was when they'd done it long ago. Something was missing.

"Still, they collected rain. And when they were done, they put the buckets of rain in the garage, where they hoped it would stay for whenever they needed it."

"What'd they collect it for?" Veena asks, so enthralled with the story that she's gripping her own knees, wide-eyed and a little flushed. "I mean you. What did you guys collect it for?"

Naomi and I look at each other. Alone we don't have all the memories, but between us there's something like an answer.

"They really didn't know," I say. Veena nods, like this nonanswer is enough. She wraps some of her necklace chains around her fingers, and I think maybe she wears them the same way we collected the buckets of water. A little unsure of the why, but positive that it is the right thing to do. "Anyway, they kept the buckets there. And sometimes, Elodee and Naomi would sneak down and stick their fingers in the water, making waves in it. They never went down together, though. They only went alone."

Veena's face falls a little. She wants the buckets of water to have changed everything, I think. She wants there to be a solution to the way we hurt.

But I don't think things are like that, outside of Eventown.

"It didn't fix everything," I say, as gently as I can. "But that one moment, when Elodee saw Naomi running in the rain after so long not seeing her smile or laugh at all—that moment was the most joyful moment of Elodee's whole life. The end."

"And they all lived happily ever after?" Veena asks when the story's done. She's hopeful, I guess, that I just forgot to say the words.

I don't answer, though. Neither does Naomi. We look at the ground. We know that's not how these stories work.

"That's the story of your happiest moment," Naomi says. She's thinking hard. I can see it on her face.

"But there's sad things in it," Veena says.

"Yeah," I say. I'm thinking hard too. "I guess there are. But I think maybe—I think it's the sad things that make it so happy?" The words don't quite make sense coming out, but they feel true anyway.

"I'm glad you held on to that story," Naomi says. It sounds like it's hard for her to say.

I'm glad I held on to the story too.

"See what I mean?" I say. "We need the rest."

Naomi doesn't agree, but she doesn't disagree either.

Veena speaks in a voice so quiet I wonder if maybe she doesn't want to be heard at all. "The Welcoming Center is closed at night," she says. "It's usually locked, but, um, usually people who work for the town have the key."

"Like Mom," Naomi says, as if she's been thinking it all along.

"Like Mom," I say.

And we don't have to say any more words, because we know without discussing it that we are going to get that key and we are maybe, maybe, maybe, going to find our stories.

"Rain buckets in the garage," Naomi says, sort of astounded, still, by the idea, by the story, by the fact that I remember anything at all. And maybe by the fact that she has little flickers of memory, too, deep below the surface. "It sounds nice."

We don't say anything else.

We don't have to.

34

Bloom by Bloom

At midnight, it's still raining and Naomi and I are out in it, so wet I don't remember what dry ever even felt like.

Veena said she'd meet us at the biggest rosebush, and we all know, without saying it, that the biggest rosebush in the yard, the biggest rosebush in all of Eventown is the one we brought with us from Juniper. I stare at it now and try to remember the story of the rosebush. There must be a story of the rosebush. I don't think we would have dragged it all the way here if there hadn't been a story of a rosebush, just like I don't think I would have wanted to make a jasmine—olive oil cake with white chocolate—pear frosting if there hadn't been a cake story. But the stories aren't there.

All that's left is the empty feeling of missing something I once knew.

All that's left is the way my heart beats in anger at the not-knowing, at the missing.

"Do you remember—" I start, for the hundredth time probably. And for the hundredth time, Naomi sighs.

"Maybe we shouldn't do this," she says.

"But at recess—"

"You want stories because you remember some," she says. "If you didn't remember any more stories, you wouldn't need any more. You'd be like me. Like I was before the rain. I think the rain would stop. I think the flowers would shrink back down. I think our house would look like the regular houses. I think the town would go back to normal."

The town now isn't normal at all. Weeds are everywhere. They are poking out of the rain-slick sidewalks. They are brushing up against buildings. The weeds aren't the only thing that have moved beyond our house. The vines are growing all over the other houses and trees and buildings, and roses all over town have grown to ridiculous sizes and taken on beautiful new colors.

At least, I think the colors are beautiful. The rest of the town thinks they are awful.

"Roses are meant to be red," I heard Mr. Fountain mumble to himself today.

The town is an explosion of color and growth and normal things made strange and pretty things made wild and perfect things made unpredictable. It's sort of a wonderland.

"I like the town like this," I say.

"The story you told me made me sad," Naomi says.

"I thought you said it sounded nice."

"It did." She pauses. She takes a big breath. "But the niceness made me sad. We're here now. I don't want to miss out there." She pauses, like she doesn't know how to say the next thing.

"Naomi—" I start, but she shakes her head.

"No, I don't want to know anything else. I changed my mind. Stories are just things that used to be happy once. I don't want any stories, Elodee." Her face breaks open, a whole world of feelings floating across it until she composes herself again. "I want blueberry pie and to play the cymbals and to eat the same three ice cream flavors and to hike to the top of the Eventown Hills and listen to waterfalls and do a good gymnastics routine and be like Betsy and her moms. I don't want to be all complicated and weird and stuff. I don't want to be like . . . like . . ."

"Like me," I finish for her.

She won't look at me.

"Don't go tonight," Naomi says. "Go tomorrow. Tell your stories to Christine and Josiah. Let them go. It

259

will feel better. I promise. You won't have to tell me any more stories about rain buckets hidden in some garage somewhere far away. I don't want to know about things like that. It hurts. And I don't want to hurt anymore. Not even for a second."

Naomi doesn't wait for me to answer, and that maybe makes me the most angry, the most lonely. She hangs her head and turns to the house, to the vines and the way they wrap and weave around each other. She doesn't look back at me or the roses or the rain.

The rain beats down harder after she's gone. I go inside and sit at the kitchen counter, watching it all from the window. The lightning and thunder come faster, and the sound of thunder makes me miss my sister. It makes me miss my sister from a long time ago, who I remember in tiny sparks of stories—reading books in bed with me, building blanket forts with me, climbing onto a beam for the first time and falling right off, looking at me to make it better.

I miss the something else too. Or the someone else. I don't know. The thing that made Naomi and me make sense. I miss feeling whole, which I think is how I used to feel. Now I feel all full of holes. Holes where the stories used to be, and holes where something else used to be too. A love that I don't know what to do with anymore. A family I used to be part of.

A belonging. But not the way Naomi wants to belong. A different kind of belonging, that came with mistakes and it being okay to not fit in anywhere else but in my old home in Juniper.

The thunder is so loud it hurts my ears. The lightning is so bright it lights up all the strange things happening to Eventown. Veena is nowhere to be found, and I'm starting to feel like she's not coming. Every minute that passes is lonelier than the minute before.

The loneliness twists and turns. It stirs itself up, like a really good cake batter, turning a bunch of ingredients into something brand-new and delicious, except the loneliness turns into anger and the anger spins and stirs itself into rage.

Rage with nowhere to go. Rage without any stories that tell me why I might be angry. It's an awful, hungry, aching sort of anger. I'd punch a pillow if one were out here. I'd yell at Naomi if she hadn't left me all alone.

There's nothing out here to punch and no one to yell at. I turn around looking for somewhere to put the way I feel, and what I find is the Juniper rosebush. It's sitting there, taller than the others. Thornier too. With shinier leaves and softer petals. The most beautiful rosebush in all of Eventown.

But, like me, it maybe wasn't ever meant to be here at all.

Dad's clippers are lying nearby—Mom's always reminding him not to leave them outside—and I pick them up. He's shown me how to use them before, but I'm not very good at it. Especially when I'm so upset.

That doesn't matter right now, though. I attack the bush with the clippers. I tear it apart clip by clip. Slowly at first, like I'm testing it to see how it feels. Careful to avoid the thorns. Then faster, not worrying about if I get hurt or what anyone will think, or why I'm doing it at all. I tear it all down, the whole rosebush, bloom by enormous bloom.

And when I'm done, I drop the clippers and I'm breathless and empty for a really good moment.

My palms forget to hurt for a second.

I forget to hurt for a second.

But when I look up at what I've done, it all comes back. Worse than before. Now I have to miss that last little bit of home too. My palms hurt and my arms are bleeding and the rosebush is gone and I'm all alone in the rain in a place where rain shouldn't ever be.

That's how Veena finds me, ten minutes later, or maybe a hundred minutes later.

"I'm all broken," I say. "I'm all wrong."

She sits next to me. She smells like the rain. Or maybe the rain smells like Veena? I can't tell anymore.

"Are you crying because of everything you remember?" she asks. I'm scared she's going to leave me all alone too.

"No," I say. "I'm crying because of everything I can't remember."

35
Hallway of Past Heartaches

It's a wet, messy, stumbling walk to the Welcoming Center. Veena and I hang on to each other and I wish Naomi were with us, too, but I try to focus on nothing else but getting where we need to get. Mom's Welcoming Center key is in my pocket, and Veena asks me every few minutes if I still have it. We're both nervous, I think. And nervousness is new to Veena. It doesn't quite fit her, like a dress from the dress-up trunk we used to have back in Juniper, filled to the brim with Mom's old clothes.

I tell Veena a story about the dress-up trunk to pass the time, and she likes it. She likes all my stories, even the ones I can't quite remember all of.

"I know some stories," she says when we're almost there. The rain has slowed to a drizzle for the moment. It's such a light mist that we're in no rush to get out of it.

"You do?"

"Well. Sort of," she says. "I have these. They're not as big as stories. Mom calls them sparks. 'All we have left are these sparks,' she says."

I'm not sure what Veena's talking about until she pulls out her collection of necklaces, hiding from the rain under her shirt.

"My mom never totally let go," she says. "My dad didn't either. They gave up all their stories, but they found a way to keep a tiny bit of the past around."

I look at the collection. Dozens of charms. "Each one is a spark of a memory," Veena says. "Not a whole story. Not much. But a little tiny spark."

"What's this one mean?" I ask. I pick up a silver one that's a shape I don't recognize. It seems extra-heavy now that I know it's a teeny-tiny bit of a story, right out in the open.

"That one's India," Veena says.

"Do they remember it?" I ask. Veena plays with the necklaces, and the charms make a sound like wind chimes.

"Not much," she says. "But some of the town—there are people who want to remember more. The ones who

265

interrupted you at the Welcoming Center, like my mom. They want their stories back. A few families carry little sparks with them. Just enough to remember that there's something worth remembering."

I hadn't thought much about the other people who were with Ms. Butra that afternoon. It hadn't occurred to me that I was part of a whole group of people who weren't so sure about all of Eventown's rules.

"There's always something worth remembering," Veena says. She raises her eyebrows. It's a little mischievous. A look I haven't seen on Veena's face before.

There are so many parts of Veena I've never seen. There are probably parts of Veena that Veena has never seen.

She squeezes the charms in her hands. The one of India must leave a mark on her hand. An outline of a spark of a story.

I want to hear about every charm.

I want to hear every story.

It's only a few minutes before we reach the place where all the stories are locked up. I haven't been to the Welcoming Center since the day I got interrupted here. We circle the building, to make sure no one's there watching it. We're all alone, though. The rest of the town is asleep, dreaming, probably, of a sunny and perfect Eventown day. We try the key in a few different doors, and it doesn't work until the very last one. It fits perfectly into that door, the one way in the back. A small black door that almost looks too small for normal people to walk through. But the key clicks and we duck our heads and walk inside.

It's dark, darker than anywhere else in the whole town. Veena takes my hand, and we let the sound of her necklaces hitting each other be the only noise. We feel for something—a light switch, a flashlight, some tiny bit of light that can guide us. But for minutes upon minutes upon minutes there's nothing. Finally when we've walked down what feels like the longest hallway in the world, we reach what I think is the room Naomi and I first entered into, the welcoming room with the banner and cake and the cozy fireplace.

I know we can't start a fire in the dark, but I remember the room had a pretty chandelier, too, hanging high above us. And I know there must be a light switch for it some-where. So Veena and I split up and follow the walls of the room, until finally, with a *whoop!* Veena hits something that makes light fill up the room. It's a warm light, a quiet light, the exact right light for this space. It's the kind of light that makes you want to curl up and give away all your stories, I guess.

"Wow," Veena says.

"What?"

"I've never been here."

"You haven't?" I ask, surprised until I realize of course Veena hasn't been here. Veena doesn't have a Before.

"It's pretty," she says. "Comfortable. Like a home."

"It felt like home," I say, "being here. It felt safe."

The word haunts me now. Today the Welcoming Center doesn't feel safe at all. I'm scared of everything hidden here and everything we are deciding to do.

But Veena looks calm, so I focus on her face and look around for clues of where to go next.

"Where do you think they keep the stories?" I ask.

"Could be anywhere," Veena says.

"Then I guess we better get to work."

I lead Veena into the storytelling room first. It lights up when we walk in, a few candles flickering themselves into light. The surprise makes me jump, and Veena jumps too. I have a hundred questions already, but I know Veena doesn't have any answers.

"This is where we told stories," I say.

"I've heard about this room," she says. She touches a few things that maybe she's read about in Eventown textbooks—the couch, the chair, a blanket, a pillow. I look for something else, for some trunk or closet or drawer where they put stories. Nothing in the desk. Nothing in the closet except for a coat and a broom. Nothing in the bookcase but more blank-paged books. I even push at the wood carving of the rose on the wall. It's smooth in some places and rough in others. It looks like it's been here forever, and I love the way it looks like a promise. I imagine Jasper Plimmswood himself carving it, imagining his fresh start.

Walking from the bookcase back to the couch, however, I notice a creak in the floor. It's a sort of shudder, an almost-lump under my foot that could be a wrinkle in the rug, except in Eventown it seems like rugs don't wrinkle and floors don't creak.

"Veena," I say. "Come here." I kneel on the ground and pull up the lavender rug. Veena gets distracted for a moment with how soft it is to the touch, but she helps me lift it up. Underneath is a brass panel, big enough for a person to fit through. The panel is textured, but when I lean in close—very close—I see that the texture is actually tiny engravings of names. Hundreds of them, too small to read many of them, but I see an Arthur and a Maria and a Nancy and a Jamal.

There's a tiny knob in the right-hand corner of the panel. I try to twist it this way and that, but it doesn't budge. Veena hovers over it and grabs the knob, giving it a pull up and out instead of a twist.

The panel comes all the way off, and we teeter over

what is now a big open hole in the floor.

"Wow," Veena says, her voice mostly breath.

I peer down the hole. There's soft lighting coming up from wherever the hole leads. A ladder made of Eventown vines swings below us, begging us to climb down it.

Except we have no idea what we'd be climbing down to.

"What do you think?" Veena asks. She lies on her stomach and brings her face over the hole in the ground, as if the extra few feet will let her see what's down there.

"The stories could be at the bottom of the ladder," I say.

"What else could it be?"

"I have no idea," I say, because it feels like I know nothing about this place anymore.

It's Veena who knows how to be brave right now. It's Veena who takes the first step onto the vine ladder. And it's Veena who says, "It's okay, Elodee. We can do this."

Her necklaces make their ghostly wind-chime sound, and I follow that noise and my friend down the vine.

It's a long climb. The ladder swings back and forth with every step, and my hands start to hurt from gripping the leaves and branches. But I'm grateful for the pool of light below us and the storytelling room still visible above us.

After minutes that feel like hours, we reach the bottom. Except the bottom is nothing but a hallway of doors. The doors come in every possible color and material. Stained glass. Bright-red rubber. Shiny gold. Doors made of sheer silk and paper and brick and thick wool. The doorknobs are different too—shapes of different flowers. Not Eventown flowers. Not roses. The doorknobs are shaped like flowers that only started appearing after things got strange here. Daisies and tulips and lilies. Sunflower doorknobs and pansy ones too. All the flowers Dad's shown me over the years. All the doors, in fact, seem to be made of things that I haven't seen in Eventown. There are beautiful paintings on the doors, and there was no art in Eventown that I can think of. One door looks like it's made of the pages of a book—one with actual words in it.

"Look," Veena says, and I look above us. Hanging from the ceiling are all kinds of objects, things that look like they came from other lives, from faraway places where things go wrong and things hurt and people make mistakes. There are diamond rings and old keys and baseball mitts and china plates and locked diaries. There are ties and wedding gowns and graduation caps and maps of places I've never been before. And there are books. So many books. "What in the world is all this stuff?" Veena says. We are both spinning around with our faces turned up, trying to take in every last detail.

"They're sparks," I say, suddenly sure. "They are sparks of stories, little tiny bits and pieces of memories."

I want to see something that I recognize, something from Juniper, but I don't see anything familiar. It's probably where Dad was supposed to bring his rosebush. And maybe the photograph of him that's hidden in my bedside table drawer. Anything that could remind us of something else.

These objects all belong to other people, though. Maybe people who have stood on the sidewalk by our house and looked at us like we don't belong. Maybe people who have suggested that we might want to leave.

We try all the doors, but each one is sealed shut, as if it was never meant to be opened ever again. I feel a rush of sadness at what could be locked inside there. Doors lead somewhere, and locked doors with no keys seem wrong. I have a feeling that there are more objects like the ones hanging from the ceiling inside, more sparks, more bits and pieces of the world outside Eventown.

The hallway seems to stretch in front of us forever.

"Maybe we're in the wrong place," Veena says. But I feel sure we are in the right place. There are sparks of stories all around us. Some out in the hallway, some locked behind those doors. Now we just need to find the stories themselves.

"I don't know what we're looking for," Veena says. She sounds frightened, like her former bravery has flickered out along with the candles upstairs. It's my turn to be brave.

"I think we'll know when we see it," I say. None of the

doors seem right. The flowers on the knobs, the shape and size of them don't look like they hold stories.

Until we reach the last door. It is a dark, unfinished wood. And etched into the wood is the same beautiful rose carving that hangs on the wall in the storytelling room. I'd know it anywhere. "This one," I say. "This is what we've been looking for."

Veena leans in close. She tries to open the door, but it doesn't budge. Her eyes search the surface for some hidden button or latch. Instead she runs her finger over the center of the wooden bloom. "There's words," she says. She brings her face so close to the carving that her nose is almost touching it.

"Wow," I say. "It just looked like scratches to me."

Veena shakes her head. She squints. "'The Hallway of Past Heartaches,'" she reads, before letting out an enormous exhale from the effort.

"Oh," I say. "Well." Because words aren't enough to respond to the pain of that title. A whole hallway of everything that hurts. It sounds like the kind of place most people would try to avoid. But Veena and I push and pull at the doorknob. Following Veena's lead, I lean in close to it, looking for clues. There's a very small keyhole. But we don't have the key.

"Shoot," Veena says. "I wish I knew how to pick a lock."

"I know how," my mouth says before I have a chance to catch up. But once the words come out I know they're true. Someone taught me. I focus hard on the image coming up in my mind. A pair of familiar hands. The same hands that taught me how to cook taught me how to pick a lock.

"I need a bobby pin," I say. "Or something small and narrow like that."

Veena runs a hand through her hair, but neither of us has any bobby pins or barrettes today. It's too bad Betsy and Naomi aren't with us. They always have their barrettes.

"Oh!" Veena says after a moment. Her hand moves to her neck. Of course. With dozens of necklaces on, there must be one that is the right size and shape for this lock. I help her look, pulling the chains apart, inspecting each charm. A horse. A half heart. A leaf. A raindrop.

Then there it is. The last charm, the one closest to her skin. A tiny sword.

I'm dying to know the story behind it. I want to know what spark it holds, what it means. But right now it has a more important use. She unclasps it from her neck and hands it to me. I stick the tiny point into the hole and move it around in circles and jabs. It's familiar. I've done it so many times I don't have to think about it. I just wish I knew when and why and with who.

It doesn't take long for the lock to unhitch, for the knob

to turn, for the door to open.

"How did you—" Veena starts, but she knows I don't know the answer.

"Before," I say, because it's the only answer that makes any sense.

The room that's revealed is pretty dark, but I rush inside. Veena moves slowly.

"Do you hear that?" she asks. I don't want to be quiet and listen for something. I want to look around. But her voice shakes, so I still.

"No, what?"

"That," Veena says, rolling her eyes to the ceiling, to the town above.

The sound is quiet but distinct. Bells. Loud ones. The kind that usually hang in enormous churches and only call out on Sundays.

"Pretty," I say.

"No," Veena says. "I mean, yes. But no. It's the alarm."

"The alarm?" The bells get a little louder. They don't sing out a song. Of course they don't. There's only the one song.

"I don't know what it's for," Veena says. "It's never gone off before. Only for drills. But when we hear the alarm, we're all supposed to meet up in the pre-designated location."

"And where's the location?" I ask.

Veena bites her lip. She closes her eyes. She keeps hugging herself, like she might fall to pieces otherwise. "Here," she says at last. "If the bell goes off, we are all supposed to meet right here. At the Welcoming Center."

36
Half Orange, Half Peanut Butter

It takes a long minute to take in what Veena's said. The whole town is coming here. Quickly. The scared part of me wants to climb up the ladder and join them. That part of me wants to pretend we've done nothing out of the ordinary today.

But the other, bigger part of me takes over. "Well then," I say. "We better move quickly."

It turns out it's hard to move quickly here. Because inside the room is another collection of doors. These doors all look like the door we just entered, though. Except for their sizes and shapes. There are small circles and huge triangles and every possible size of rectangle. Every single one of them made from the same unfinished wood, roses carved into the surface.

This time all the doors open. And inside each new, smaller room, we find what we are looking for. Shelves. Shelves that, I'm sure now, are piled high with stories. On each shelf are dozens of wooden boxes, carved with roses just like the doors themselves, with names engraved on their outer edges. There are hundreds of boxes, and a quick glance tells us they're in alphabetical order. And that each little room is for a different letter of the alphabet. We count the doors. Twenty-six of them.

"Oh," Veena says. "Oh, wow. It's really here. Stories. The whole past. Right here."

"Right here in the middle of Eventown," I say. Veena runs her hands over the boxes, mumbling names to herself. "Randall. Renson. Rodriguez. Rogers. Ryan."

I duck into another room, with a zigzag-shaped door. "Farrell. Faul. Feingold. Fence. Fenton. Flint. Forrest. Nope, this isn't the right room," I read out, loud enough for Veena to hear even over the sounds of the bells.

"Try the next one!" Veena says. She sounds frantic. I run into another room, a circular-doored one. She follows me. "Aaronson. Abrams. Applebet," I read.

"Applebet?" Veena says.

We both pause. Only for a moment, though. The bells are insisting we move faster.

"I'll leave it out," I say. "In case she wants to listen."

Veena's eyes widen, but she nods.

The B's are right next door, and we find Veena's family's boxes, one for each of her parents. We pull them out too. We don't know what to do with them, but we know they belong to us. Those stories belong to Veena's family.

Finally, we find my room. It is a room with the smallest square door, and we have to crawl inside. "Lenox. Lester. Lilith. Lively. Here we are," I say. "Lively."

"It's a good last name for you," Veena says, like she's really thinking about it for the first time. The bells ring out louder still. I can't imagine how loud they must be out on the streets.

I take Naomi's box instead of my own. I need to know which memories Naomi treasured most, so that we can remind her. Then I'll listen to my own. When I'm a little less nervous.

The box is feather-light when I pick it up from the shelf. And when I open it I can see why. All that's inside are six tiny speakers with six little gold buttons on top.

"Do I press one of them?" I ask Veena. She makes herself even smaller.

"Okay," she says.

I don't know what else to do. So I press the gold button marked *Joy*. Then I wait for whatever's going to happen to happen.

There's a scratchy pause.

Veena reaches over and presses the button again. The scratching stops.

"They're almost here," Veena says. "We can stop now. Maybe we should stop now. Before we change everything."

"I thought you wanted to be here," I say. I swear I can hear voices entering the Welcoming Center. Footsteps maybe. Only a few, but they're coming.

"Maybe we're better off not knowing anything," Veena says. Her voice shakes. She has to speak loudly to be heard over the bells. "So much has changed already. Maybe everything that's happening outside is a sign of something terrible and dangerous and wrong."

I close my eyes to help me think. Sometimes I think better when I can't look around a room or look at someone else's face.

Finally I shake my head.

"Everyone's so scared of the rain and the growing flowers here," I say. "It doesn't make any sense. Things are growing. More colors are showing up. More seasons are coming. There's *more* here now, not less. So why is everyone so scared?"

"It's different," Veena says, but she doesn't sound so sure.

"I like how the flowers look," I say. "Even the weeds. I like them. They seem like someone finally set them free."

"That's what my mom said they were trying to do," Veena says. "I heard her talking to her friends about it. About interrupting your stories. She said if they timed it just right, maybe they could set you free. She said if you were set free, maybe things would change here."

"She said that?"

Veena considers. I can tell she wants to say it just right, but there isn't time. "They like to pretend it's very solid here," she says. "But it's not. It's fragile. Even my necklaces scare people. Mom's jalebi too. And the butterfly house. If we remember the wrong thing . . . well. I guess this happens."

She says *this* and I know she means the rain and the flowers and even her own heart shifting and shaking and growing more wild inside of her.

"How do you know?" I ask.

She pauses. There's a secret no one's told me, and I can see it on her face and even in her fingers. "It happened before," she says. "Not like this. Never like this. But a family came, and they brought along this wagon. This red wagon. And their Welcoming got stalled, because one of them got scared. And it didn't rain or anything, but it got hot. And that other thing. The sticky, wet feeling?"

"Humid?" I say.

"Humid," Veena says. "It got hot and humid until they

finally agreed to finish their Welcoming and tell all their stories. Christine and Josiah said we fixed it just in time. That's what I've heard, at least."

"What family was it?" I ask.

Veena pulls me past more of the L's. She pulls out a box. "Ludlow," she says. "Betsy's moms."

We pull the box out, but we don't listen. I hope, though, that maybe they will. Maybe they'll let me listen, even. Maybe I'd understand them better if I could.

The bells ring louder. We need to listen to a story. One story. The right story.

A story to help us remember what we are here for. A story to help us remember why Eventown might not be so perfect after all.

I go back to Naomi's box and the six gold buttons inside.

I press the one marked Joy.

"Once upon a time"—Naomi's voice rings out as if she's right here with us—"there was a boy named Lawrence."

Veena pauses the recording, just as my heart is pounding at the name Lawrence. "Why is she talking like that?" she says. "We need stories from her life, not from a book or something."

"That's how they had us tell hard stories," I say. "Like they belong to someone else."

Veena looks sad at the answer, but she nods and presses

the button again. Naomi's voice continues. It's shaky. I wish I could hug this Naomi, the one telling the story.

Upstairs, there are definitely voices now. And a pounding of footsteps. A town's worth of them. They haven't found us yet, though. "Lawrence was cute. Nice-looking. Everyone said so. He looked a little like Naomi and Elodee and a little like Mom and Dad. He was—I'm sorry, do you need all of this? I can just get to the point."

Josiah's voice interrupts the recording to answer her. "You can tell us everything you remember. The more the better. We have all the time in the world."

There's a pause and I can almost see Naomi nod. "Okay," she continues. "Well. Let's see. Lawrence liked to do a lot of things. He liked to garden. He liked to sing. He liked to bake."

The voices and footsteps draw closer, so I can't stop the recording again, but my mind swims and my heart pounds and I say the name Lawrence in my head a hundred times in one single second. A little piece of my heart breaks open. I know that name. I know a boy named Lawrence who loved to bake.

Just like me. I turn the volume up on the recording. I beg the people upstairs to stay away long enough for us to finish.

"When Elodee and Naomi turned eight," Naomi's voice

says, growing a little less shaky, "Lawrence made a cake for the first time. Lawrence was fourteen, which was a pretty good age to make a first cake. He wanted the cake to be half orange for Naomi, who loved oranges, and half peanut butter for Elodee, who loved anything peanut butter.

"The cake was disgusting. It was wet in the middle and the orange and peanut butter tasted all wrong together. On the top he wrote the twins' names, but it was hard to fit all the letters, so they trailed off to the sides, making the top look like it said *omi and Elo*.

"'I guess that's what I'll call you from now on,' Lawrence said. 'My little sisters, Omi and Elo.'"

The recording keeps going, and Veena is listening, but I don't have to. The spark of story has opened up the rest of the memory for me. The names fit. Naomi thought the names fit even better than our real names, plus they were better because Lawrence had come up with them. I can hear him calling me Elo right now.

It makes my heart flip. Then ache.

I know that Lawrence and I were super close, and sometimes Naomi felt left out. She wasn't as loud and brave and silly as Lawrence and I were. But on our eighth birthday, Lawrence pulled Naomi—Omi—aside. He told me to stay put. That he needed a little special time with Omi.

They went out to the backyard, and I watched them

from the kitchen window, just like I watch the rosebush from the kitchen window now. I watched Naomi teach Lawrence how to do cartwheels. He was awful at them. His legs were too long, and he always started laughing halfway through.

I remember it began to rain while they were out there. I remember I walked away from the window. I never liked the rain very much. For me that's the end of the memory, but Naomi's voice is still talking, so I turn the recording up to hear what I missed after I left.

"Omi walked to the door when the rain started. But Lawrence stopped her. He told her they could try cart-wheels in the rain. He joked that he'd probably be better at them that way.

"Omi wasn't so sure. It was muddy and messy and even sort of dangerous. But Lawrence did one first, and he fell down, mud splattering everywhere. Something about the way he laughed made Omi feel like it would be okay. So she stayed out there too. Doing cartwheels. Making a mess. Slipping and falling. It was weird, but she liked it. She liked it way more than she ever thought she would.

"'You're wonderful all the time,' Lawrence told Omi. Told me," Naomi on the recording corrects herself, the story hers for only one minute longer. It tugs at my heart even more. "He told me I was best of all in the rain. We stayed out there all afternoon. Just the two of us. No Elo. No Mom and Dad. Just me and Lawrence. Both of us loving the rain together.

"And it was just ours."

There's a pause on the recording. A big sigh. The unmistakable noise of Naomi fidgeting. Then her voice, small and sad. "That's the most joyful story I know."

37

Sometimes a Spark Is Enough

I'm crying.

And Veena is crying too. I don't think she's ever cried before. She wipes the tears from her face and looks at her fingertips in shock. "Oh," she says, over and over. "Oh."

They scare her. "Make it stop!" she says, but I can't.

"You're crying," I say. I huddle next to her. I let her cry on my shoulder, the tears coming so fast she can't wipe them away anymore.

"It's so wet," she says. She hiccups. She tries to breathe normally but can't. "It's hard to talk! Why is it so hard to talk? And breathe? And *stop*?"

"You're sad," I say, rubbing her back the way Mom used

to rub mine, I think, back when I was in Juniper. Back when I used to cry too. "You're sad for all of us."

"It feels bigger than sad," Veena says.

"Yeah," I say, remembering something but not everything. Remembering only the edges of the way sad felt, because sad is locked away in my box. "It's like that sometimes."

For a moment, it's easy to ignore the voices getting closer, the never-ending bells, the footsteps as they parade through the Hallway of Past Heartaches.

"A boy named Lawrence," I say.

"You had a brother," Veena says.

"I had a brother." It breaks my heart, to have to use the past tense. I hold my breath, wishing I could make it present. Wishing I could make him present. I don't know what happened to him, I don't know where he is, but I hate that I forgot him, even for a moment. I hate that we all forgot him.

"They made you forget," Veena says. She's still sad, but it's a different sad now. A sad with some anger mixed in. Some bravery. Some certainty.

I nod.

The door to the tiny room we are in swings open.

Dozens of townspeople are there, on the other side. The rest, I'm sure, are upstairs still, waiting for normalcy to be restored.

I don't think it will be.

I hope it won't.

"Elodee!" I hear my mother cry out.

"Veena!" Ms. Butra says.

"What are you doing?" Naomi says. She is huddled next to Mom, so tight nothing could possibly fit between them. "Elodee. What have you done?"

"These are ours," I say, gesturing to the shelves of boxes holding years and years of stories. "It's time we took them back."

Veena is nervous next to me. The tears have thrown her. The dozens of people at the doorway have thrown her, and I think learning about Lawrence has thrown her too.

Josiah and Christine are shaking their heads near the back of the group, whispering urgently. Probably discussing what they're going to do with us.

But the story of Lawrence, Naomi's story of Lawrence, has made me braver, so I go on.

"I want to remember everything," I say. "Even though it will hurt. I want to know all of it. The good parts and the bad parts and everything else. I want to know all the parts because they're all—they're all mine. And Naomi's. And Lawrence's. They're our stories."

Veena nods. She clears her throat like she wants to make sure her voice comes out as true as possible. "No one should ever have to forget a story like that," she says.

"Does anyone else want to listen to their stories?" I ask. I pretend this is normal, because so far no one is rushing at me and prying Naomi's box from my hands. No one is yelling at me. No one is telling us to stop.

They are all in a stunned silence. They look at the ceilings, at all the objects that might even mean something to some of them. They look at the rows of stories. But mostly they look at me and Veena and our tears. I go on. "I loved your story, Naomi. About Lawrence and the rain." I watch her face for a sign of remembering. "Will you listen to mine?" I want to sit side by side with my sister and listen to all of our stories and tell any others we can think of. I want Mom and Dad there too. And anyone else who wants to listen. But mostly I want to know what else Naomi loves and aches for and wonders about. The things she misses about Lawrence aren't the things I miss about him. We don't miss him in the same way. And missing might even mean something different to both of us.

Christine finally emerges from the crowd of quiet, confused spectators.

"Okay," Christine says. "All right. Now. This can all be put back together. It can. You listened to how many stories? One? Two? And did you listen to your own or someone else's? Did Veena here listen to her parents'? If we know exactly the damage that's been done I think we can put things back together the way they're supposed to be."

"We listened to one," I say. "But we want to listen to more."

There's a grumble, at last, among everyone watching.

"We want to listen too!" Ms. Butra says. She makes her way into the room with us. She puts a hand on my shoulder, and one on Naomi's. More women and men, the ones who stopped my Welcoming, join us too.

"I want to listen," says a woman in a beautiful silvery hijab.

"I want to listen," says a man with a thick mustache but a bald head.

"I want to listen," says a woman with long braids.

"I want to listen too."

The last voice is one I know.

My father.

He joins us in the room, too, his shoulders back, his face a little flushed, his eyes only on me.

"I told you," he whispers in my ear, "that day when you brought me pancakes, that if you ever wanted to remember, it was okay. I told you it would still be there, if you needed it."

That day wasn't very long ago, but it could have been another lifetime. When he said those words, I didn't know what they meant. Now I know.

"I never totally forgot," I say. "Not everything."

"If you remember one little thing," Ms. Butra says, "it can be enough to open the door to the rest. And Elodee held on to three stories. Sometimes a spark is enough. And sometimes a whole story can change everything."

"Everyone calm down," Christine says. Josiah hasn't come forward yet. He is wringing his hands in the back. "Let's all take a deep breath. Ms. Butra, with all due respect, what you did in the middle of Elodee's Welcoming was completely inappropriate. And our lack of following up was also unacceptable. I'm not sure how we missed that. Josiah is usually very good at keeping our records in order. We've all made some mistakes here. But it's okay. We know what Eventown is for, don't we?"

I look back at Josiah again. He has a funny look on his face. A little like a smile. Ms. Butra is looking at him too. I'd thought he was worried, but he's not. He's excited. He's excited that something is happening.

I see Ms. Butra mouth something to him.

Thank you.

He catches my eye. And he blinks. It's a long blink that goes along with a long nod.

His own box of stories, I see at last, is in his hands. He holds it close to his heart.

I mouth *thank you* to him too.

"Why are we here in Eventown?" Christine calls out

again, more desperately. "Aren't we here to have the best, happiest lives we can?"

I look to the crowd, waiting for their nodding heads. But their heads don't nod. They are confused and bewildered and surprised. They are wandering in the hallway and into other rooms. Some of them, maybe, I hope, are looking for their own stories already.

"What's the true purpose of our beautiful town?" Christine tries again. She wants them to call back something about a fresh start.

They don't.

We don't.

There is another ruckus, more people climbing down the vine ladder, a few families arguing about what to do about their stories, and people asking me what I remember. In the middle of all of it, Naomi and Mom hold hands and crinkle their foreheads and seem to be stuck in a moment of not-remembering and not being sure if they want to remember.

But I need them to. I need them to remember Lawrence. My brother.

"We want to listen," Veena says, her voice so clear the whole world quiets to hear it. "We hope you do too."

Veena pulls my box of stories from the shelf.

She hands it to me. Gives a nod of her head, telling me

it will be okay. So I hit the gold button marked *Heartbreak*.

"Once upon a time," I hear my own voice say. And I sit down on the ground. Because I can tell from the way my voice shakes that it is going to hurt.

38
What Lawrence Forgot

Once upon a time, there was a boy named Lawrence.

Most little kids asked for toys for Christmas. Lawrence's friend Alex got a train set. His friend Bryan got a science kit. His friend Sandra got a basketball hoop.

Lawrence asked for only one thing—a rosebush.

His little sisters would be arriving soon, according to his parents. And Lawrence had fallen in love with flowers. He liked ones that other people called weeds, but still seemed beautiful to him. He loved flowers in vases and in fancy gardens and in people's hair and coming from trees. He begged his parents for a rosebush. He promised them he'd tend to it himself.

Lawrence's mom and dad got him that rosebush. It couldn't

fit under the tree, of course, so they tied a ribbon around a single rose, and when Lawrence saw it he looked at them with wide eyes and wonder.

"Look outside," his dad said, almost as excited as Lawrence himself. Lawrence jumped up and ran outside and there it was—the rosebush. He yipped. He cheered. Then he made a big mistake—he ran up to the rosebush and hugged it. Mom and Dad shouted when they realized what he was doing, but it was too late. Lawrence had been poked with the roses' thorns. Luckily, only a few had dug all the way into his skin, but it was the first time Lawrence had to go to the emergency room nonetheless.

Other kids might have been scared of the rosebush after that, but not Lawrence. Lawrence loved it and tended to it and spent hours sitting and waiting, hoping to watch the moment the blooms opened into grown-up roses.

When he got older, Lawrence kept at his gardening. He planted vegetables and herbs and all kinds of flowers. But his favorite thing in his garden was still the rosebush. He wasn't afraid of getting a little bit hurt by something he loved so much.

Sometimes Elodee and Naomi helped Lawrence with his garden, but neither of them took to it.

Eventually Lawrence started up cooking, too, and the two interests worked well together. He grew herbs that he could cook with. Every day after school, he'd work in his garden, and in the evening he'd make delicious things in the kitchen, and he seemed happy most of the time.

Except sometimes Lawrence wanted to stay in the garden instead of going to school. Or anywhere else.

Sometimes he left a recipe halfway through.

Sometimes Lawrence decorated the whole neighborhood with flower wreaths cut from his garden. Sometimes he'd wear a rose or a daffodil pinned to his shirt.

But sometimes he didn't do any of his wacky and wonderful things. Sometimes he hid in his room and said he was tired, and his roses would start to look tired too.

When Lawrence was sixteen and Elodee and Naomi were ten, Lawrence looked tired almost every day.

Elodee tried to be wacky and wonderful enough for the both of them when Lawrence hid away. She wore silly outfits and sang on the bus and even baked the things Lawrence loved to bake. She'd bake peanut butter–banana cookies and apple-cinnamon-blueberry bread. But the one thing she couldn't bake without Lawrence was his specialty cake. Lawrence's specialty cake was one he'd made up himself when he was having one of his hard weeks. It was a jasmine–olive oil cake with white chocolate–pear frosting. And it was delicious.

Whenever Lawrence made the cake, he'd start to feel better. The cake, he said, was like magic.

Elodee wished she could make that magical cake herself.

Maybe when she was a teenager herself in a few years, Lawrence would teach her how. But Lawrence stopped baking altogether over the holidays, and he didn't start back up again in the new year.

Naomi and Elodee asked him to. They begged him to make angel food cake or pick some flowers and arrange them in a vase. They asked him to play Monopoly or watch a movie or go on a bike ride. They asked him to just sit at dinner with the family, to be there.

He said no.

He said no to school and to his friends wanting to go on a ski trip and to Mom and Dad insisting he go to the doctor. He said no to getting out of bed and eating food and talking.

"It's called depression," Mom and Dad said, when Lawrence said no to Naomi and Elodee's birthday in April.

"But Lawrence always bakes us a cake for our birthday," Naomi said.

"He can't this year," Mom said.

"But Lawrence loves our birthday," Elodee said.

"Sometimes he forgets how much he loves things," Dad said. He stared at the rosebush. It was starting to droop.

"Has he been forgetting for a long time?" Elodee asked. She was thinking of the day Lawrence didn't join them at the beach and the day that Lawrence gave up on his specialty cake baking halfway through and Elodee had to finish it without him.

She still couldn't get the special cake right without him, even though she was sure the magical cake would cheer Lawrence right up.

Mom and Dad looked at each other. They didn't like Elodee's question. It made them sad. Dad shuffled his feet on the floor. Mom kept her mouth shut very tight. Her fists too.

They didn't answer, but Elodee was pretty sure not answering meant that Lawrence had been forgetting for a long time and that maybe Mom and Dad didn't know how to make him remember.

Elodee and Naomi tried to make him remember. They knocked on his door to bring him a rose plucked from the bush and a batch of sugar cookies that Elodee had experimented with, adding lavender and basil and a scoop of raspberry jam.

"What do you want?" Lawrence called. He sounded tired. Maybe he just needed someone to help him wake up. Cookies were good for that. So were twin newly eleven-year-old sisters.

"We brought you flowers and cookies!" Naomi said.

"We thought we could play cards. Or go for a walk. Or just eat cookies in your bed. Can we eat cookies in your bed? We won't be messy! We brought napkins," Elodee said. She was getting excited. This would work. Lawrence would remember he loved cookies and flowers and his family.

"Not right now," Lawrence said. He sounded even more tired.

"But I made the cookies especially for you," Elodee said. She wanted to fling the door open and tell him everything he'd forgotten—that his new patch of tomatoes was coming in and that Naomi had perfected her back flip and it was the best thing ever to watch her nail it over and over, and that Mom had bought Elodee and Lawrence a special torch to make crème brûlée and Elodee wasn't allowed to try it out without her big brother's help.

"Your rosebush is getting sick. It needs help. And Dad's really bad at helping it," Naomi said.

"He'll figure it out," Lawrence said.

"I don't think he will," Elodee said. "When do you think you'll come out of your room?"

"Tonight?" Naomi said. "Mom said we could have burgers and eat them outside tonight. She said maybe you'd take us out for ice cream after."

Lawrence sighed.

It was a big sigh.

Naomi would say later that it sounded like the ocean.

Elodee would say no, it felt like an earthquake, shaking the whole house.

Lawrence didn't say anything else. His sigh told them to leave him alone, to forget about him, to stop trying. Naomi and Elodee leaned against each other and stayed outside his door for half an hour, then an hour, then two, hoping he'd smell the *cookies or the rose or their eagerness and love and come out and join them.*

He didn't.

They ate a quiet family dinner without Lawrence. It didn't feel the same as a family dinner with Lawrence. There were no hamburgers, and they were not outside. They ate leftover pizza inside at the kitchen counter while Mom and Dad took turns getting up to talk quietly on the phone with a doctor.

"Maybe it will be better tomorrow," Naomi said.

But it wasn't.

Because tomorrow Lawrence was gone.

Mom picked Elodee and Naomi up from school early and told them in the parking lot. She meant to wait until they got home, but when she saw them she began to cry, and the words came out all on their own.

"Your brother took too many of his pills and he got sick and we weren't able to make him better. He went up to live with the angels."

"Angels?" Elodee asked. She didn't know much about angels. No one had ever told her much about angels.

"I want him to live here, though," Naomi said.

"All our memories of him will live with us," Mom said, her voice all strangled and strange. "And where he is, he'll be safe now. And happy."

"He used to be happy with us!" Elodee cried. She threw her

backpack across the parking lot. The sound wasn't nearly loud enough for what she felt.

Everything stopped that day, the day that Lawrence forgot that he loved the world.

39

The Stories Inside

By the time the recording ends, there's not a whisper in the
crowd. Even Josiah and Christine have their heads bowed.
Like the tale of Lawrence, like this piece of my past—this
piece of my present, this piece of my heart—is sacred.

Betsy and her moms have joined us downstairs, and they
lean against the walls. Naomi has joined me and Veena and
the box of my memories. Mr. and Ms. Butra are standing
by Mom and Dad, and about a dozen other residents have
huddled around us, reaching arms to our shoulders, offering
looks that are between smiles and frowns.

The silence is long. No one wants to be the first to
break it. Some of the residents have tears on their faces.

Others look frightened. A few look like they want to escape back upstairs, like memories might be contagious. Like heartbreak might be contagious too.

And maybe it is, because of all the crying and the way people aren't just hugging us, but they're hugging each other.

"Tell us more about Lawrence," Baxter says. I hadn't noticed him there, with Maggie and Victor, watching and waiting and finally being brave enough to be the first one to speak. I hadn't known Baxter could be brave. I had been feeling like I was the only brave one, all by myself. But now there's brave Veena and brave Baxter, and even Naomi being brave in her own way. She stays right by me. She doesn't close the box with all the buttons containing all my other stories. In fact, she holds her own box and opens it up, staring at the stories inside.

I close my eyes. Now that the one story of Lawrence has been told, others come rushing back at me. It feels like they've been there all along, hiding somewhere dark and dusty and sad, and now they're thrilled to be back on the surface of things.

All they've ever wanted was to be told.

Naomi, Veena, Ms. Butra, Mom, Dad, and I step outside the little room and into the Hallway of Past Heartaches, where at least fifty people are gathered. I am not the only one ready to tell more stories. Many families have found their own boxes and are nervously tapping their fingertips on the buttons inside, playing with the idea of pressing them.

Ms. Butra is the first to do it, and I hear her voice from many, many years ago ring out. *They called me names*, her voice says. *I missed my home and they told me to go back there.*

I can't hear her story, though, because so many other buttons are pushed. I think I can pick out Ms. Applebet's voice, talking about hiding in a closet when her father was angry, and a man from our street, Roshan Dweck, finding cruel words written on his home in spray paint one afternoon. *I thought we were neighbors*, the voice says.

There's Mr. Fountain's voice, which sounds the way mine sounded, speaking of Lawrence. I think I pick out that he had a brother, too, and that his brother also died. I hear Mom and Dad telling their own stories of the day Lawrence died and Mr. Butra telling a happy story about expecting a new baby.

We walk through the Hallway of Past Heartaches, and there are heart-joys too. Snow days and birthday parties and weddings and new jobs and laughing so hard your stomach hurts. If I listened I could hear about hospitals and loneliness too. People deciding to get divorced. Secrets being kept. Delicious Thanksgiving dinners and afternoons lost doing nothing but staring at the ocean.

When Naomi finally presses another of her buttons,

more memories of Lawrence come back to me—him making crepes every day for a month, Lawrence fostering a puppy one week until our parents found a home for him. Lawrence yelling at Mom and Dad to leave him alone. Lawrence abandoning his special cake halfway through, and the sad, gooey mess in a bowl on the counter that Naomi cleaned after a few days because Mom and Dad seemed too sad to do it themselves.

Lawrence as he was—sometimes lifting us up on his shoulders or chasing us around the front yard, sometimes hiding under the covers.

I loved every version of him. My big brother.

I still do.

Naomi, Veena, and I hold hands and walk farther down the hallway, pausing to listen to some stories, hugging people who seem like they might need it, laughing along with ones who need that.

We pass Betsy and her moms. They are gathered around Betsy's tall mom's box of stories. She is hovering a finger over a button and looks afraid to press it. But her wife and Betsy both tell her she can do it, it's okay, it will be okay.

When she presses it, I know her story is a sad one too. *Once upon a time there was a girl named Sabrina. She loved her parents. But they only loved some parts of her. When they found out about the other parts, they sent her away,* her recorded voice says. Betsy sees us and we know it's okay to stay and listen. So we do.

We listen even though it's hard.

And when the listening is done, Betsy and her moms walk through the hallway right behind us.

There is so much to listen to. So many things to learn about so many people.

The stories are hard to hear and fun to hear and scary to hear and strange to hear. We are messy, listening to them. People cry and hide their faces and make new noises they've never made before and laugh louder than ever before too.

And also. They hold each other. Some by the hands, like Naomi and I start to do, and some around the waists or shoulders. Some are in tight hugs and some in loose, gentle ones. Some are leaning their heads together, making pretty triangle shapes between their faces.

They make new shapes. Ones I haven't seen before in Eventown.

"No one really touched anyone else here," I say to Naomi. "Look." And she does. She looks out at the crowd, at everyone who's been angry with us and disappointed in us and also sad for us and listening to us. We've seen them shake hands and kiss cheeks before. But we've never seen them hug. We've never seen them wipe tears from one another's faces or cradle each other or smooth down strands of hair, rub backs, rock someone who isn't a baby back and forth, back and forth.

"They all love each other," I say to Mom and Dad. "I hadn't noticed before."

"It was hard to see," Dad says. "Love has a lot to do with imperfections. And Eventown doesn't have many of those." We draw closer together as a family. We know a lot about imperfections.

A man comes down from upstairs and looks at what is happening in the hallway. He points at me. "Look what you've done," he says. "It was her, wasn't it? It was that family. You ruined us!"

I can hear more shouts from upstairs. Maybe they are angry, agreeing with the man. Or maybe some of them want to come down and join us and our memories.

Because Eventown doesn't look ruined. Not even the crying, messy, aching people around us. They don't look ruined at all. The man doesn't stop his yelling. But Dad doesn't apologize and neither do the rest of us. I think I've seen the man before around town, wearing his fedora, riding a bike. But I see him differently now. I wonder if he was born here or somewhere out there, where hard things happen. I think I see in the wrinkles on his forehead and the crack in his voice that he has stories too. That he came here to get away from them. That all those stories are locked in a pretty wooden box right here, a few feet away, and he's afraid of them.

"It's raining outside!" he says. "It's chaos! My wife is crying. My kids are upset. Nothing's how it's supposed to be. Nothing's in order."

Naomi takes a big, brave breath. "Love is messy," she says. And maybe the man hears her and maybe he doesn't—Naomi's voice, even at its loudest, is quiet, and the rain is still drizzling outside and someone else's story is playing.

No one's smiling right now, listening to a sad story about losing a job, but we're all together. It doesn't look sunny and beautiful and perfect. It's so much better than that.

Dad sees it too. So does Naomi. And Mom, still crying over Lawrence, still hanging on to Dad's arm like it will save her from the way she feels; she sees it, too, I swear.

Love, in the way we take care of each other when we're hurting.

Love, in a town covered in vines and thorns and roses and color.

Love, strongest in the worst, scariest, most painful moments.

Love, even better when the sky is gray and your heart is breaking.

40

Twins on the Outside

"We won't forget you," Mom says to the vine-covered house. We are standing outside it, the four of us. Our car is back, packed to the brim with everything we need to move back to Juniper.

"We'll have a lot of stories to tell about this place," I say, and Mom squeezes me tight. More tightly than she's squeezed me since Lawrence died. I think for a long time Mom thought loving too hard would just make her sadder. And maybe some days it does, but it makes her happier, too, I think.

It's weird, how you can be happier and sadder at the same time.

I said that late at night, too, the evening after we listened to the stories at the Welcoming Center.

"You're both happy and sad right now?" Dad asked. I nodded.

"Mad too," I whispered, because I was so tired of all the things I hadn't said. "At you."

"And at Mom," Naomi said. I was surprised to hear her chime in. But relieved too. I wouldn't be saying everything alone or feeling everything alone.

Or remembering everything alone.

We talked for hours that night. Long enough for me to make three different kinds of hot chocolate and long enough to move from crying to laughing to yelling and back to crying again. Long enough to tell one hundred stories about Lawrence.

At first, Mom's mouth puckered over his name, like it didn't taste right.

At first, Dad had to clear his throat five times before every story, like it was stuck somewhere in his chest or belly.

But long, long past our bedtimes, his name got easier to say. The memories came fast and eager; we couldn't tell them quickly enough. For hours we only told the good stories, the ones where Lawrence laughed and teased and frosted perfect cakes and invented new kinds of tacos and had garden dirt under his fingernails and a gleam in his eye.

But eventually, we told the harder stories. The sad ones. The confusing ones. The stories where Lawrence was unhappy and quiet and telling us to leave him alone.

We choked a little over the worst parts.

But.

The stories were easier to hear when Mom told them than when I told them to myself alone in my head. The stories were easier to bear when Dad breathed them out than when I was trying and failing at forgetting them.

I could curl into Dad's side.

I could watch Mom's face and see she was still there, she was still Mom, even when it hurt.

I could tell half of a story and Naomi could tell the other half, and it was better to unwind it all together.

"If we'd been better at talking like this with Lawrence—" Dad said in a moment of quiet. He didn't need to finish the sentence. We all knew the end. Mom put a hand on his arm. She shook her head.

"We did our best," she said. "And he did his best. And it's not anyone's fault."

And that much I knew was true. That we all did our best. Mom never complained about the messes in the kitchen, and Dad asked Lawrence a billion questions about flowers and plants, and when Lawrence wanted to be alone we sometimes tried letting him be alone and we sometimes tried making him be with us, and we worried and wondered and waited and wished.

There's an ache in all of us, I think, where we wish we'd talked more about how hard it all was. And the ache will make us talk more now about the things that hurt or confuse or twist us up inside.

But an ache isn't the same thing as guilt. An ache doesn't mean we were bad sisters or parents or people.

An ache is just an ache: something that settles into your heart and reminds you that love is there even if the person you love isn't.

"I'm so sorry," Mom said, and I think she meant for everything. For Lawrence. For Eventown. For the long silences and the way his name became a bad word. For the things we didn't say and the things we were afraid to feel and the places we didn't want to go.

Naomi and I didn't say *it's okay*, because it's not okay, exactly.

It's something else.

It just is.

"We were scared," Dad said.

And it was the truest thing I'd ever heard.

And in that moment, I finally really got it.

There's a flaw in the Eventown system. Feelings cross

all over each other. There can't just be one gold button for joy and one for grief and one for fear. Sometimes you're all of those things at once. Sometimes you're scared of being sad, or sad about feeling happy. Sometimes you're nervous about something you love or embarrassed by everything stirring around inside you.

Sometimes you love the way a place has rosebushes and perfect sunsets but are scared of the way those things make you feel. Sometimes you wish you could forget, but you're actually happier when you remember. Sometimes you are angry with your parents but hopeful that it won't last forever.

We all slept piled together in the living room that night. I don't know when we fell asleep. I don't know when talking turned to dreaming. But when we woke up, we knew we'd be going back to Juniper. Even though it felt scary. Even though it felt sad. Even though we were a little angry with Juniper and the things it took from us.

Somehow, even with all those feelings, it was also home.

Still, as we get ready to leave today, I know I'm going to miss the way the wind smells and the perfect ice cream cones and maybe even the anthem. I'm going to miss making perfect fried chicken, even though it will be more fun to make imperfect fried chicken.

Dad notices the way I have scrunched my forehead at all the dozens of feelings buzzing around me at the same time.

"We can visit," Dad says.

"But only for a few days at a time, right?" Naomi says.

"A few days sounds right," Mom says. "A few days is all you really need, I think."

Naomi walks toward the house and I go to follow her. She turns around and shakes her head.

"I want to do it alone." She tucks a strand of hair behind her ear. She doesn't look so much like me after all. Her eyes are sadder and her back is much straighter. She's got muscles where I don't have anything and her hair is starting to curl at the ends. Mine doesn't do that. "Let me say goodbye my own way."

I let her go into the house alone and I go into the backyard and the place where the Juniper rosebush used to be. I'm a little sad that I ruined it, a little sad that it can't make the journey back with us. I wonder—I can't help it—what Naomi's doing in the house, and I feel a pinch of sadness not to be part of it, to have to be sad in my own way, in my own space and time.

I find one single rose bloom near where the bush used to proudly stand. I'm not sure, I can't be sure, if it's from the Juniper bush or one of the Eventown ones. But it's a full red bloom, brilliant and way too big. If I hang it in our

315

bedroom, upside down, it will drain and dry and become something fragile but keepable. It's not the same as a rosebud growing on a bush. The colors will shift and the texture will go papery and if I slam the door too hard or Naomi's feet knock it over when she's practicing a handstand it could go to pieces.

But memory is like that, I guess. Not quite the same as it was when it was alive and happening. Delicate. Something you have to care for, tend to, love gently, and hang on to as hard as you can.

I almost take one for Naomi too. But Naomi probably doesn't need a dried rose to remember Eventown by. Naomi isn't sad about the same things I am. We won't miss the same things, or the same people.

And the lonely part of me wants to miss the same things and know and love the same things. But the other part of me knows Naomi is right. We have to say goodbye in our own ways.

Not just with Eventown.

When Naomi comes back to the yard, she finds me with the bloom in my hands. "Pretty," she says.

"Your happiest memory," I say. "I didn't know all that."

"Yeah," she says. "Sometimes when you talked about Lawrence after he was gone, I felt like I didn't know him at all. Like you were describing some person I'd never met."

"That's how I felt hearing your memory. That's not what I remember about him."

"Maybe that's okay," Naomi says. "It's like how you get angry and I get quiet. Or how you want to stand out and I want to fit in. Maybe we loved Lawrence in different ways. And knew different things about him."

"Remember when Lawrence said we're only twins on the outside?" I ask. It's the first time Naomi's let me continue past the words *remember when* in so long. It feels good to get the whole sentence out. The whole sliver of a memory.

Naomi grins. "Yep."

"He was right."

"He was right about a lot of stuff. And really wrong about other stuff."

It's a true and small and achy sentence.

"You girls need anything else?" Dad calls out to us. "Or is it time to hit the road?"

I remember that there's one thing inside that I want to take with me. One thing that someone brought with us, from Juniper to Eventown. And it's only right to bring it from Eventown back to Juniper.

"One second!" I call, and run into the house, up the stairs, to the bedroom I shared with Naomi. Somehow it doesn't feel like ours anymore. I go to the nightstand and open the drawer. It's there, inside, where I've been keeping it. The photograph I thought was a young version of Dad.

It's a photo of Lawrence. Of course it is—those are his red cheeks and his sneaky smile and his big hands and his light, sad, happy eyes.

He was here with us this whole time.

I put it in my pocket, then take it back out. I don't have to hide it anymore. The photograph of Lawrence can be right in my hands; it can be framed and put on the mantel or glued into a scrapbook or put in a locket to wear around my neck.

I know, now, that we can talk about him. That we will talk about him. That we won't hide him away or let ourselves think of him only when we're alone in our rooms.

"What'd you get?" Naomi asks when I get back to the front lawn. I show her. Lawrence isn't a secret to hide away. He's our brother.

The sun is rising. The sky is golden, and at home I'd want to soak in every second, because I'd know it will disappear soon and become just the regular daytime sky. But here I almost forget to look. I almost forget that it's special or beautiful or worth noticing at all.

We both look at it in silence for a few minutes. It doesn't shift. It doesn't start to turn into another color. The clouds don't even move in the sky. And there's no more hint of rain.

Still, I bet if we described it, we'd describe it differently. Maybe even call it a different color. Maybe it's yellow to Naomi, or dark silver, or light orange.

But to me, right now, it's golden. And I want to remember it. I want to remember every moment of it. Even after it's gone.

41

A Very Sweet Cloud

We drive back up and over the Eventown Hills. They look smaller, driving over them from this way. Greener, too, from all the rain. The smell of roses is just as strong. It follows us as we move out of town. Veena and her parents have a car behind us, and every so often Naomi and I turn around to wave at Veena. She looks scared. She doesn't know what life is like over these hills.

We'll help her. But we won't tell her not to be scared.

Soon, Veena will have answers to all six of the Welcoming Center questions. She'll have a most embarrassed moment and a most heartbreaking one.

But Veena's going to have a most joyful moment too.

And if I know Veena, it will be huge and vibrant and fun and filled with her special brand of bravery.

I hope I get to be there with her. I hope I get to be there for all of it.

When we're all the way over the hills, we wave at them. Veena does, too, from her car. We wave at the pine trees, at the blueberry bushes, and the roses, at the still golden sky.

Our old Juniper house has new owners, so we stay in a rental on the edge of town near Veena and her parents. It's far away from the things we knew best—the mall and Bess's house and the familiar path to school. It's a small house, and messy too. We won't be here forever.

But for now, it's sort of nice to be on an adventure. An adventure that doesn't take us somewhere perfect. An adventure that brings us somewhere where lots of things can go wrong.

The lawn isn't covered in rosebushes, but there are dandelions growing here and there, and we can make wishes on the wispy bulbs. Veena and I sit down right away and blow the delicate weeds into the wind.

Veena's never done it before. There's so much she hasn't done before, and I'm excited to show her the world outside of Eventown.

Naomi doesn't sit with us. She can't resist the long, flat

expanse of yard. It's the perfect place to do gymnastics. She starts with a cartwheel, then a walkover, then a round-off back handspring. She trips coming out of it and falls backward with a little yelp.

Veena gasps. But Naomi only laughs.

"Guess I better get back to practice soon," she says. She tries again and again, the old joy coming back. Sometimes the back handsprings are pretty good and sometimes they're sloppy, but they're somehow better than they've ever been. She makes up a routine on the spot.

"For Lawrence," she says, and it's goofier than anything she's done before. Sillier and dancier and messier. She's a different kind of gymnast than she was in Eventown, of course, but she's a different kind of gymnast than she was before Eventown too.

We could watch her for hours.

But I have some baking to do.

The kitchen is nothing like the Eventown kitchen. The stove is old, but not the good kind of old. The counters are narrow. The light above the counter is too dim and there aren't pretty copper canisters of flour and sugar. There's a tiny window, but it looks out at the street, not at a rosy backyard.

Still, I know for a fact that it is good enough for a cake.

Veena and Naomi walk to the store to buy my ingredients for me. Naomi wants to sign up for gymnastics and Veena wants to see roads with potholes in them and trees without leaves and whining dogs and cars honking at each other at busy intersections.

All I want is to remember.

I prepare the kitchen for the cake. I butter and flour pans. I cut parchment paper. I take out measuring cups and wash the grime off the old metal teaspoons I find in a drawer. I put butter on the counter to soften, and I smile when Mom turns on some music.

The Beatles are playing our favorite song.

I close my eyes to the tune and remember everything I can. I let it all come to me—the happy things and sad things. And by the time Veena and Naomi return with grocery bags of white chocolate chips and fresh pears and jasmine tea, I'm ready.

"You need help?" Veena asks. "We can do it together."

But Naomi and I exchange a smile. For once, we're thinking the same thing.

"No," I say. "I'm okay doing it on my own."

I grab a bottle of olive oil. A sprinkle of jasmine. A crooked pear. An overflowing cup of white chocolate chips, stealing a single one to taste.

It tastes like a very sweet cloud.

It tastes like magic.

This time, I can feel Lawrence next to me, baking with

me, reminding me when to add salt, how to whisk sugar into frosting, how long to let the cake do its magical growing in the oven.

He reminds me to trust it, not to check on it. Opening the oven door too early could ruin everything.

I wait.

And when the cake's out of the oven, it's golden brown and smells a little like a garden.

I have to wait, again, before putting the frosting on. The waiting is hard. I want everything to be delicious all at once. I want to skip over the hard parts, the boring parts, the lonely and sad and angry parts.

But if I do that, the cake won't be good. It won't be right.

So I wait. Even though it's uncomfortable and too hot in the kitchen. Even though I don't feel like waiting for the good part.

While I wait, I think about the summer coming up and what it will be like. I think maybe I'll learn how to garden, like Lawrence. But I think I'll do other things, too, things that Lawrence never did and Naomi's never done. Maybe I'll take piano now that I'm not afraid of music class. Maybe I'll learn all the songs we weren't allowed to play.

Maybe I'll make up some of my own.

The possibilities are endless. It's going to be a good summer. I can already feel the hum in the air, even though it's only the beginning of May. Last summer, we didn't do much of anything. The memory makes me sad. It hurts all over again.

This time, though, I know it's supposed to.

Finally, the cake has cooled and it's ready for its finishing touches. I start frosting it. It's fluffy and sweet but not too sweet. It tastes a little like white chocolate and a little like pears and a little like something else—the magical space between the two.

I spread it all over the cake in twirls and swirls that are off center and messy and sometimes all over the counter, my face, the floor.

When it's done, I call everyone to the kitchen. I take out plates from the cabinet. They are regular plates. White and boring and chipped in spots. I cut slices for Ms. Butra and Mr. Butra and Veena. For Mom and Dad. For Naomi. For me. The slices are all different sizes and some of them fall over. There are crumbs absolutely everywhere. Globs of frosting too.

But when we each take a bite, it's a strange taste, a sad, sugary, complicated, lovely taste.

It's Lawrence's cake. But mine too.

"Lawrence would have loved this," Naomi says.

It's a sad sentence; a sentence that makes us miss him a little bit more.

But like the cake, the missing is a little sweet, too, a little wonderful, a little sad, a little messy and crooked and delicate and strange.

A little like Lawrence himself.

We eat the whole delicious thing.

ACKNOWLEDGMENTS

First and always, thank you to my agent, Victoria Marini, for seven wonderful years of working together and finding new ways to tell the stories I want to tell. You are my rock in this industry.

Thank you to my editor, Alex Arnold, for pushing me and inspiring me and never letting me off the hook. Thank you for everything we share and for getting me and my brain sometimes better than I get myself. Thank you for a lovely and incredibly special collaboration that makes my books and my life better.

Thank you to Katherine Tegen for continuing to support honest stories and for helping my books find the readers who need them. I'm so grateful to be part of the Katherine Tegen Books family.

Thank you, Rebecca Aronson, for your thoughtful feedback on drafts of this book, and for all the ways big and small you contribute to bookmaking magic.

Thank you, Alana Whitman, for being a lovely light in this publishing journey, and Rosanne Romanello for all your support. A special thank-you to Robert Imfeld and Gina Rizzo for helping this book find its space in the world.

So many incredible people put amazing work into my books, and I want to especially thank those who make the messy beautiful and the written word visual: designer Aurora Parlagreco, production editor Bethany Reis, copyeditor Maya Myers, and illustrator Jane Newland.

Lots of thanks to my family and friends who make the challenging parts easier and listen when there's nothing else that can be done.

Thank you always to my husband, Frank, who lets index cards and Post-it notes and piles of paper take over the kitchen table for months at a time. Especially with this one. I love you.

And thank you to my daughter, Fia Frances, for being one more extra-special reason to tell stories.

ALSO BY
COREY ANN HAYDU

KT KATHERINE TEGEN BOOKS
An Imprint of HarperCollins Publishers